COME AGAIN?

By Paralee Keys Hoot

ISBN: 0-75963-873-X

This book is printed on acid free paper.

1stBooks - rev. 6/07/01

Chapter I

How happily we step inside, Expecting to be free;
And find, instead, the changing tide
Presents a snarling sea.
Pkh

Peter Newman walked to the edge of the pool and sat on the concrete bench at the diving board end. The water was sparkling, clear and faintly colored by the aqua green coating of the pool walls. The circulating pump was working, and eddies of waves beckoned as they broadcast a tart scent of chlorine. He sighed. How long, he wondered, would it be before he had to shut off this exotic sight? How had the picture changed from a promise of security to the possibility of watching his dreams transferred to the finance company that carried the note.

He smoothed their crumpled letter reminding him that a substantial payment would be expected at once. FAT CHANCE! He scrunched and hurled the letter into the pool. Then, like an old, old man, he got down on his knees to retrieve it.Pete was more than a little concerned about the future of his inheritance. Surely a late twenty year old man with a college degree could reverse the threat of bankruptcy. Scanning the three buildings snuggled neatly together amid the landscaped garden and enticing pool, he did a mental assessment of the sixty units, including the thirty that were vacant. THERE JUST HAD TO BE A WAY TO PUT THIS PLACE INTO THE BLACK. He'd find it. He WOULD! Energized by his resolute musing, he stood and started toward the laundry room, just in time to notice an unfamiliar figure striding toward him.

"Good afternoon. Are you the manager?" The man's voice was friendly and matched the six feet, two inches of well-exercised body. His slick, black hair, as well as the brown eyes, suggested a Hispanic heritage. His flawless English indicated an educated background.

"Yes. I'm Peter Newman." The words followed his outstretched hand. "How can I help you?" He sucked in his stomach and hoisted his hundred and sixty five pounds to its ultimate height. He still lacked an inch or so being as tall as the newcomer.

"My name is Charles Reasoner, better known as Chary for some reason." A manicured hand gripped Pete's outstretched one. "Your sign says you have a vacancy. Do you?" The question inferred he had been turned down some time in the past.

"Glad to meet you, Chary. How many do you need? Upper or lower? One or two bedrooms?" Pete chuckled.

Chary joined the humor. "ONE will be sufficient. Do you allow dogs and kids?"

When Pete's answer was slow in coming, Chary added: "Not that I have either. Just inquiring." His wide grin showcased flawless incisors.

"Well, no. Actually, we've kept this an adult area, and if you produced one, I hope you would stick around long enough to raise it." He frowned. "You look familiar to me. Do I know you from some place"?

"Funny you ask that. I was just wondering the same thing. Strange how a thought can employ two separate minds at the same time, isn't it?"

"Yes, it is. Mental telepathy, I suppose."

They were standing near a vacancy, toward which Pete used his left hand like an arrow pointing the way. He opened the door and stepped back for Chary to enter. He liked this guy's playful humor. It was akin to his own, even to the way Chary went through the apartment, opening closets and drawers, trying out the mattress, and checking the space in the refrigerator. Everything about him is like an echo of what he would have investigated. Pete opened the tailored drapes at the living room window, allowing the view of the garden area to complete the selling job for him.

"This two bedroom is six hundred a month with a three year lease and two month's deposit up front. We require references, which we check. There are other, less expensive units I can show you, if you like? Parking for this one is directly behind the unit in a security fenced area.

Chary stood looking at the pool area, his private thoughts hidden behind his next words.

"May I see the lease?"

"Certainly. Let's go to the office." Once more Pete stepped back and indicated the direction by an arm gesture, his thoughts forming his opinion of the inquirer.

'Probably wondering if a man of mixed race would fit in,' he surmised.

"Would you like to see another unit? Upstairs, perhaps?"

"I rather like this one. May I see the lease?"

"Certainly. You know you really do look familiar. Do I know you from somewhere?"

Chary let out his contagious chuckle again. "If not, I am sure we will get better acquainted if we become neighbors. Where do you live, by the way?"

"Right next door to you. if you take this unit. Sure you want this one?" Pete grinned.

"OH Man!" Chary slapped his forehead and laughed, but he gave the room another approving look as he followed the landlord out and into the office. Once there, he took the proffered chair and glanced at the interior decor while Pete opened the file drawer to produce the lease form.

"What is your business, Chary?" Pete pushed the form across the desk.

Chary answered the question before starting to read it.

"Like everyone else in the world, I am a computer analyst and instructor by day, and I do a bit of bar tending by night. What is your other job?"

"Touche!" *Pete shook his head and laughed "I spend full time trying to keep the bills paid on this place and don't always do a great job of that."*

Chary looked up from the lease from and teased. "Maybe you should use a computer to help you manage?"

"Did you say you are a computer analyst or salesman?"

Charles Reasoner, the computer analyst, grinned and read the lease with a thoroughness expected of a man of his occupation. With one manicured finger on the item concerning 'next of kin', he protested.

"I am not in my parents' good graces these days. I'd like to skip that one if it is not a legal requirement. OK? I can give you as many personal and business references as you need, though. Will that be sufficient?"

Pete's eyebrows shot upward. "Fair enough". He quipped. "I was just thinking that here I am, an orphan with adopted parents and wondering every day who my birth parents were; while you have parents from whom you try to escape. Let's see your deposit check, and I'll show you the parking space and the laundry area and get a key for you to move in as soon as your check clears. Is that OK with you?" Pete did not bother to control the sneer that could be heard in his voice.

"Whoa. I wasn't trying to dodge a question. And I don't mind telling you why I don't choose to have my father's name listed as someone to be called in an emergency. He is one of those determined people who thinks his plan for his offspring is THE ONLY way to go. I left home in order to get my own life going. What he had picked out for me just wasn't my idea of a life." Both men were silent for a moment; then Chary quipped, "When CAN I move in? Are you sure I don't know you from some place?" His humorous quip was too friendly to be ignored by such a slight disagreement.

"Oh Man!" Pete groaned, and shook his head in like wit. After all, this might be the one that opened the gate to greener pastures. It could be the beginning he had been seeking. Maybe his fortune had started to improve at the instant he made that decision to find an answer. He watched as Chary signed the form and made out his check for the amount required. All tension faded from the encounter as he took his new tenant on a tour of the place. After the tour, they were back by the office door.

"Chary, feel free to look the place over as long as you like," Pete offered. "I need to stick close to the telephone, but I will be in the office if you need me. Glad to have you as a neighbor." Chary's response was wrapped in a friendly smile as he put his hand forward in agreement.

Other apartments were rented, even while Chary wandered about the grounds. More followed in the next week, and, by the end of the month, there were but six vacancies. Pete was ecstatic. His latest ad was producing results.

Not that everything was that pleasant, though. Number twenty was carping about her air conditioning. Still thinking about his oldest resident, he retrieved a towel from one of the lounge chairs and headed for the laundry room, his thoughts continuing to berate his pet peeve, Mrs. Strickland, his inherited assistant manager.

Boy! She is an example of harassment for you! He could not remember when he first became aware of her as a part of his life. She had always been there. Because his mom was too ill to take him, Mrs. Strickland had taken over the duty of escorting him on his first day of school as well as other maternal duties when his father was too busy to do so. She did a lot, he reminded himself, but she was intolerantly bossy. As far back as he could remember, she had acted like his overseer, and he resented it.

"I remember the time, though, that she ran out and picked me up when I fell off my new bike," he muttered aloud. "Even then she had to lecture me. I might have liked her if she hadn't always been so BOSSY. As it is, we're caught in a situation neither one of us can stand, and there is nothing either one of us can change. Even at this minute, he fancied he could hear some of those love songs from the forties and fifties that she constantly played. Pete's clenched fists caught his attention. He had not realized he was talking to himself, and the knowledge did little to calm his outrage.

"I was just a little kid the first time I heard those records of hers," he said aloud as he pulled the pool testing kit down from a shelf in the tool room. This many new tenants necessitated much testing of the pool water for proper PH. level. That had been his first duty, and his dad had stressed its importance. Like a kid forcing himself to eat unwanted vegetables, his thoughts persisted in justifying his feelings about the old lady.

She was a size fourteen if his guess was anywhere nearly correct, and he suspected that the red in her hair came out of a bottle. Even if her comfort shoes did not blend with the garish colors she wore, he had to admit that her fried apple pies and oatmeal cookies had been a welcome part of his childhood. Pete shook his head at these conflicting emotions.

Mrs. S., as he generally called her, was still bossy. According to her, nothing he ever did was his best. She continually told him how much better he could have done. How many times had he heard her say 'Don't EVER say you CAN'T'?

Yet, when he reminded her that her rent was two weeks past due, she reminded him that she was not paying another dime until her apartment delivered cool air. It never seemed to occur to her that her rent was half of what the regular tenants paid. His father had insisted on that concession.

"I'm TRYING to get that fixed for you, Mrs. Strickland, and," he recently had said to her retreating back, and her only response was, "There is a vast difference between TRYING and DOING, Mr. Newman!"

It would be later, to his bathroom mirror, that he would think of just the right repartee. At least at that moment it felt like it would have been the right thing to say.

"I'm sorry, MRS. STRYCHNINE," he remembered himself saying to the mirror. "I will be ever so happy to assist you and your baggage out to the street so you can cool off," but, no, he never did say those things.

Well, he would get the electric bill paid and she could cool off while she wrote her check. UNLESS IT WAS HOT ALSO. He really disliked the old bag, even though she had been a life long friend of his dad. If ONLY his dad had not insisted that she be kept as the Assistant Manager when the apartments became his inheritance! He was stuck, and he knew it. No amount of home cooking could make him like her, though.

Of course, he was going to be civil to her to her face and in front of others; he was the original Mister Correct who kept calm at all costs. And that was about to change. Yessiree! He was getting this place to a paying position, and, then, he could be what his name implied, A NEW MAN! From then on, 'NO RENT, NO ROOF' would be his motto. Satisfied with his test of the pool water, he took the kit back to its accustomed place, turned off the light and headed for the office.

At his desk he ran his hand over the sleek mahogany surface that his father had loved. Under the glass fitted to its top were pictures of himself and his sister as children. His dad had been a softie where his kids were concerned. What a very long time ago those pictures were made! But he still remembered that day and how reluctant he had been to stop playing long enough for the pictures to be taken. He looked a lot like his dad in one of them, but his dad was not really his dad, at all. They had adopted him at the age of three. For the hundredth time that day, Pete wondered what his real father and mother were like.

In another corner was a copy of the original deed to the apartment complex, just a copy, not the original. That had been sacrificed to the bank when his dad was forced to put the place up as collateral for a loan to pay for his mother's illness during her last days. After her death, his dad did not exude the same measure of love and constant care in the upkeep as he earlier had done, and now that laxity was staring at his adopted son in silent reproach for having allowed the finances to grow precarious.

He opened a drawer to the file cabinet and withdrew the folder of unpaid bills. With one hand on the adding machine, and the other thumbing his way through the sheaf of papers, Pete found himself sighing again. He could not clear all of the red balances; but, perhaps, he might be able to hold things together while he collected all the delinquent rentals. He would read over those lease agreements one more time and see what his options were. He looked up as the door opened and a gorgeous female came inside.

"The sign said 'COME IN,' she reported. "Please do," Pete stood and indicated a chair by the desk. "I'm Pete Newman. Are you looking for a great apartment?"

"Yes. Do you rent that kind?"

"That's the only kind we have. Would this be for you and your husband, or ...?"

"Just for myself, thanks. I am Kelly Richardson, single, no children, and a hostess at the Colonial Country Club. I have my own furniture, and I hope you have an unfurnished unit that might be adequate for me, a two bedroom, perhaps? I have a car. I hope you have assigned parking spaces? I can afford my own rent. I'm not wanted by the police; I don't play music too loud, and I've never been asked to leave any place I've rented. Oh, and I love to swim, and your pool looks heavenly." Her smile made him think of the first encounter of a new day when the sun forced its way into his bedroom window. He didn't know they made women like this anymore!

The telephone jangled, but Pete ignored it.

"My answering service will catch it," he explained. "I'll show you what we have. Yes we can accommodate you with an unfurnished apartment. That is no problem. And we have a nice two bedroom on the second floor."

"The second floor would be nice, I think." Her smile had Pete on his feet at once. "Let's go upstairs and look at number 21. It overlooks the pool and has an east front. The only thing is, I am not sure you would enjoy your neighbor in number twenty."

"Oh? What is wrong with him?"

"It's just that SHE is sometimes nosy, and you might not care for her endless questions about your personal life, and, unless you enjoy listening to early country and western music..." That sounded dumb, even to his own ears, but there it hung with its bare face mocking him for his stupidity. Fortunately, she did not seem to be concerned by this disclosure.

"Oh, I usually have no problem in that department." She flashed her pearly whites again, and Pete was convinced she did not have any such problem.

"Fine. Let's just go up to look that unit over." He moved to the door and opened it for her to precede him. He took a deep breath of the heady fragrance that surrounded her. Motioning toward the stairway, he began to and describe the apartment they were to visit. She was probably twenty five, he conjectured. Only a woman of that age could move like the soft breeze she resembled. Definitely the product of an elite school. Her provocative smile displayed flawless teeth held slightly ajar to accommodate her mint flavored breath as she spoke. Pete was convinced that this role of exquisite sexuality had been perfected by many hours of practice.

'The east front of this unit will assure privacy for the bedroom while offering a full view, I mean, the sun won't wake you up...uh, that is to say..." Pete blew a full breath and inflated his jaws before forcing the air to exit through clenched teeth. He shook his head to clear it of the hideous faux pass. Rubbing his reddened forehead, he realized the futility of attempting an explanation. Kelly Richardson gave him a big smile to cover his embarrassment. He unlocked the door and stepped back to allow her to precede him into the apartment. Her foot happened to be occupying the space he had intended to use.

"OOPS. SORRY!" He had NEVER felt like such a klutz!

"No harm done; FORGET IT!" Her sincere understanding was emphasized by a gracious pat on his arm. Then she sealed her forgiveness with a little laugh as she added "I'll remember in the future to not attempt entering a door at the same time you are entering." What could he do but shake his head and agree with her?

Fortunately, she approved the accommodations in number twenty-one and inquired about lease agreements and contractual limits. All of this, he told her, could be discussed in the office. Again, he held the door for her to precede him, and again came that enticing hint of a mint flavored breath and subtle cologne. Her descent to the lower floor appeared to be a much practiced art. Pete noticed that her brand of confidence did not require her to look down at the steps she was taking, nor did she protect herself by holding to the stair rails.

In the office, his offer of a chair was acknowledged with a gracious nod. She sat and crossed shapely legs, made visible with the aid of her short skirt. Accepting the lease agreement to peruse, her blue eyes met his in silent acknowledgment. As she read, Pete noted the delicate way she held the paper before opening her oversized handbag to retrieve her pen. She filled in the needed data and handed the signed lease back to Pete. Then she performed the same ritual by reaching into the bag for her checkbook.

She held her check between two fingers, accentuating the provocative twist of her wrist. Nor did he miss the delicate chain cuddling her trim ankle. He would be willing to bet her clothes did not come from a factory outlet, and there was no doubt this blond siren never had to spend Saturday evenings alone; nonetheless, he sat wishing he could think of a legitimate reason to detain her.

Business concluded, she rose and turned to leave. Again he opened a door for her, and, again, her smile signaled her gratitude. He was still gazing at her sexy walk from the office when she turned and waved a friendly good-bye, proving to Pete Newman that she needed no extra schooling. He felt sure she had already graduated.

Pete returned to the desk and sniffed her check, hoping for another hint of her feminine scent. He added her check to the bank deposit before filing her application under 'R'. A knock at the door interfered with his busy thoughts. He turned his head as the knocker entered. and announced: "I'm from the IRS; can you ......?"

If he had imagined the heady aura would last throughout the day, he was wrong.

Before turning around to face the speaker, Peter Newman took a long, deep breath.

Chapter II

The race of mankind would perish
Did they cease to aid each other.
We cannot exist without mutual help.
Walter Scott

"Ooh Man! Pete's eyes closed with no help from his brain. He could feel himself growing smaller, and his next breath came with some difficulty. Standing, he motioned to a chair for this latest, and most unexpected, visitor. He pushed his right hand out and was conscious of its sudden dampness as the Agent shook it and waved away the offer of a chair.

"No, no. I am not here on an official visit. My car just died, and I need to call my office for someone to send help. Sorry if my introduction frightened you. Could I use your telephone? My cell phone won't work unless the motor is running."

Pete's relief came in long, deep breaths. "But your presence is intimidating, anyway", he thought. Glancing at his cluttered desk, he muttered:

"Certainly."

He cleared a space for the telephone on the visitor side of his desk as he moved the folder of lease agreements. To afford the intruder some privacy, Pete stepped to the doorway to wait for the call to be made. Following such transaction they met in the center of the office floor and again shook hands, this time with less moisture.

They were different types, unlike in every way. Frank Fisher was blond, short and endowed with a pallid complexion that betrayed his lack of sunshine and exercise. Probably drank a lot of coffee, thought Pete. Although the man's nails were clean and buffed, his eyes, a limpid blue, lacked the sparkle of a happy individual.

"Likely a divorced hypochondriac." Pete shrugged his broad shoulders as if the action would boost his own height. He was so relieved at the man's reason for being there that he felt downright friendly.

"Have you been with the Service long?"

"In fact, YES. Although I am not an agent, I've been in Personnel for about ten years."

"Then I take it that you like your job. Ten years is an impressive record."

Frank inclined his head in non commitment as he rose and prepared to leave.

Pete accompanied his visitor toward the street, slowing his pace as Frank Fisher glanced around the garden area.

"Yes, my work is interesting, I suppose." Then he gave a short laugh and added "but sometimes I think I would rather be a gardener, especially in a place like you have here."

"Well, why don't you just move in here with us. I have a few vacancies left.

Would you like to see one? This unit right here was leased just today, but I can show you the layout."

Seeing no sign to the contrary, Pete unlocked the door and stood aside. As usual, he watched for reaction as this possible tenant surveyed the area. This one was very thorough, likely a great person for the Personnel department. Studying people was a favorite pastime for Pete. Now he noticed that the man went directly to the window and looked out and scanned each visible area.

"What does a place like this run per month?"

"Three year lease plus two months rent in advance"

"How much per month?"

"This lower is six hundred. I have an upper on the backside for five hundred. It is a quieter unit than the lowers and the ones here in front. Would you care to see it?"

"I should not be too far away when my assistant gets here. Is it furnished like this one?"

"Similar if not better. Come on. It won't take but a couple of minutes."

Pete bent to pick up a beer bottle as they made their way to the back stairs.

"One of the lesser attributes of apartment managing." he explained.

"Don't you have a yard person?"

"You are looking at him, Frank."

Frank, the IRS personnel agent grinned and suggested a solution.

"Maybe we should make a trade. Tell you what I'll do. I will be your pickup man if you will lower the rent on that back apartment, say $100.00 a month. How about it?"

"I cannot do that, Frank. It takes 100% occupancy to make a decent living out of this thing. Besides, I do not want to be found guilty of bribing an I R S agent. And you would not want me to do that, either, I know. How about a one year lease and one month's rent up front?"

"Why not? Besides, that is not bribery, is it? That's just being friendly. isn't it? But you won't need to tell my neighbors that I'm with the IRS, will you? Maybe I can make a friend or two here. Most people dislike Internal Revenue personnel. In fact, I would not want my occupation listed even on the lease agreement. Could we handle it that way?

"That doesn't present a problem, I suppose."

" Then, let's get me signed up before my aide arrives. I think I am going to like living here."

Pete's stride was a step ahead of Frank's as they retraced their steps to the office. The lease was signed and the check had changed hands in mere minutes.

My car failure seems to have been a fortunate event."

"I agree with that," Pete offered with no further explanation. He accompanied his new tenant to the street and gave him a friendly clap on the shoulder.

Peter Newman was beginning to feel really good about things again. In fact, had he been much younger and unwatched, he might have clicked his heels together and made a wild, crazy leap into the air.

With the deposits and advance rents, he could get within sight of the green in his ledger. There was the little matter of putting deposit moneys into a separate account, but he would have to tiptoe around that a bit. Nonetheless things were looking UP, and he had no doubt whatsoever that the time to turn the tide of fortune toward himself had arrived. What a difference a day can make!

Vaguely to his mind came the admonition: "TAKE HEED WHEN YE STAND LEST YE FALL!" At that very instant Mrs. Strickland rounded the corner and headed in his direction. Why did that thought hit him just as she came in sight, he wondered.

"Mr. Newman! Mr. Newman!"

Pete stopped and walked to the door to get ready for her normal onslaught of verbal abuse. He could feel it coming.

"Yes, Mrs. Strickland. How can I help you this afternoon?"

"Have you done anything about my air conditioning?"

"I have, indeed, madam. As a matter of fact, the problem of cool air has been addressed and will be at your disposal by the time you bring your rental payment up to date."

"Humph! I ought to sue you, you know."

"I understand, Mrs. Strickland. When do you expect to bring your rent check to the office?"

"I have it right here, thank you, and I will withhold next month's check if the utilities are not sufficient for comfort. Your father never ran this place as poorly as you do. In fact, for quite a number of years my rent payment was a portion of my salary, and I haven't noticed you honoring that arrangement."

"I am well aware of my inadequate ways, Mrs. Strickland. I thank you for your check which, if you will excuse me, I will credit to your account at once. As for your rent check being absorbed by assisting my father when he needed it, perhaps you haven't noticed that I am capable of running the place without your help other than in emergencies."

"Well, I NEVER saw such ingratitude!" The petite figure pivoted and reversed her direction.

Shaking his head, Pete went to the desk to prepare a deposit of rental checks. Next, he made out a check to the utilities companies and the mortgage company. These would go into the night depository slots for early credit tomorrow morning.

"Please do not let the world end before these reach their destination," he prayed as he sealed the envelopes. Then, with a deep sigh, he muttered "Amen" and gave his head an additional shake.

Seconds later, he was starting his car and pointing it toward the bank.

Had he been less eager to make this deposit he might have kept driving. A beautiful day like this should never be wasted, he was convinced. However, it was the deposit he was delivering which made the day such a glorious one. With that thought in mind, he took no long way to the bank. He even had a hearty greeting for the teller who retrieved his deposit from the drive-in canister. His long breath escaped through closed lips as the canister flew into the air and disappeared into the teller's cage.

When it came hurtling back with a stamped receipt for his deposit, he sighed again.

During the drive home he acknowledged his relief. Although he had not retained money for his food and car expense, the deposit covered his most pressing needs, and that was a seed of happiness for him today. Mrs. Strickland had come forth with her overdue rent in time to make the deposit. Even she was on his list of blessings; what was the old saying? 'God's in His Heaven, and all's right with the world.' Well OKAY!

A moving van was parked on the street in front of the building when he returned. It could be any one of the several who were moving in this week. He did not care to be involved with their moves, but he did wonder if it might be Kelly Richardson. IT WAS! However, the convertible parked behind it belonged to someone else. Pete gave himself one guess at the occupant's identity. It could only be Chary Reasoner. He was doubly certain when he heard the cheery voice.

"Say, don't I know you from some place?"

"How are you, Chary? Getting ready to move in?"

"What do you mean, GETTING READY TO? I moved in while you were out to dinner last night."

"I did not go out to dinner last night."

"You didn't? Well, maybe you were asleep. I tried to be quiet since it was already nine o'clock. I didn't wake you, did I?"

"Not at all." Pete tried to walk past and get to his door, but he was trapped by the movers bringing in the furniture for the lady in bright red shorts and oversized tee shirt. Kelly Richardson led the way to her new apartment home, and the movers handled the heavier furniture with no evidence of displeasure at climbing to the second floor behind her.

"Wow! Is that an exhibition of female pulchritude?" Chary obviously possessed a goodly quantity of confidence in his ability to categorize the ladies. His unbelievably white teeth flashed a sensuous invitation as he evaluated the surroundings. Changing his former direction toward his unit, Chary strode to the edge of the pool where he could command an unfettered view of the new environment.

Pete inched his way around Chary and managed to insert his key in the lock of his apartment. He had no desire to make introductions at this hour. He did notice, though, that Chary did not appear to be miffed by this social shortcoming.

"Ooh, Man!" Pete muttered under his breath. Inside, he walked directly to the window to draw the shade and was in time to witness Chary's first encounter with the saucy Kelly Richardson. Although he was irritated by the brashness, he found himself grinning at the man's approach.

"Well, HELLO! Can I give you a hand?"

"Well, NO. I do not need a hand or," she gave a slight pause in her answer while her eyes did a slow trip over Chary's whole body.

"Or any other kind of help." Pete had to see the end of this opera..

Chary quickly looked at the window and noticed Pete standing there, his hands at the ready to close the curtains. It was a certainty that the landlord had seen this humiliating event. To cover his reaction, he said to her retreating figure. "Oh, I am sorry. I just thought I might have known you some place."

"No," Kelly's eyebrows rose to the top floor. "I am sure I would have remembered you." She walked away.

Pete, convulsed with laughter at this point, opened his door and motioned for Chary to join him. Maybe he should let the poor slob drown in his own pit, but this was a situation which called for assistance to the sinking man.

Chary entered and threw himself onto the sofa. "Oh, Man!" he groaned, and Pete's control completely collapsed. He would NEVER, EVER forget this priceless moment.

"Could I offer you a cold shower, perhaps?" He wiped at the laughter-induced tears.

"Thanks, but NO. I've just been iced down."

After a minute or so, Chary joined Pete in the uncontrolled laughter.

"I warned you we would get better acquainted if I rented the unit next to you," he added. "Do you believe me now?"

The ringing of the telephone motivated Chary to leave. Pete 's humor faded after glancing at the Caller ID.

"Good evening, Mrs. Strickland. How may I help you?"

"Mr. Newman. Are you aware of the noise these new tenants are making? What is this place coming to if a person cannot take an undisturbed afternoon nap?"

"We have several new residents, Mrs. Strickland. I am sure everything will settle down once they are in and unpacked. Just let me know later if you are inconvenienced in any way."

Those words seemed to be prophetic when, after the third day, peace and quiet reigned. He exchanged greetings as he met various ones leaving or returning from their places of employment, but, so far, was unable to call each one by name. He was beginning to learn which car belonged to which apartment, and he began to expect the faint sounds of running water for morning showers. So far, the air conditioner was working well, and the hot water was more than ample.

Apartments thirty-two, thirty-three and thirty-four were rented by three young lady secretaries who were employed by the same office pool and called themselves THREE PEAS IN A POD. It took little time for their fun loving neighbors in apartments thirty five and thirty six to alter that title. They were now known as THE THREE PEAS IN THEIR PADS. Patti, Paula and Pris were together always. They drove to work together each morning and returned together in the evening to disappear into separate units to change into swimsuits for a hasty swim. Popular and fun loving, they took little time to dress again and leave together for an evening out. Pete envied their energy, noting their willingness to have guests on the few times they were at home after six o'clock, P.M.

The non-stop chatter and laughter from that area amused Pete. The camaraderie was the friendly feel he wanted his apartment complex to exude. It was bound to be just such a magnetic force that would give the place an enviable reputation. Might it even induce Mrs. Strickland to move elsewhere? He laughed at such an absurd thought. He was convinced that NOTHING would cause her to leave. Her whole purpose in life seemed to be to keep him upset.

Something about the old girl worried him, though. Why was she so loud mouthed and critical where he was concerned and just the opposite when dealing with the tenants? She had been a part of his life forever, serving as the apartment manager for his father for as long as he could remember. She was part of his inheritance, and, as far as he was concerned, she was about as useful as an empty bird nest after the birds flew South. He had to admit he appreciated her watchfulness when he had to be away from the building for a little while, and she had been able to rent a few units during such absences. With the tenants, her humor and wit seemed to be a cohesive adjunct to the complex aura. Why, then, did she always leave him feeling he was about three beats off her equal status?

This older lady had been a friend of his parents, though, and he did not have the right to disregard her seniority and his dad's request. In fact, keeping her as Assistant Manager was one of the requirements if he was to become owner of the complex.

Thus far the ratio of lessors was about fifty-fifty, half singles and half married couples. It seemed natural that the couples would gravitate toward each other. Certainly there was no doubt that the singles were compatible.

Everyone knew Mrs. Strickland, of course. She made sure they did. Even the pert Kelly Richardson, who occupied the unit next to the spry senior, favorably responded to the old crone's laughter and compliments.

For as long as he could remember, she had kept him reminded of his inexperience as a businessman. She knew every person living there and was always the first to become acquainted with any who were just moving in. Well, she couldn't live forever. He'd just cope in the mean-time.

In the said 'meantime', life did what life always does. It slid unnoticed from event to event, projecting him into various predicaments and lulling him into false glimpses of security. Spring greened into full lawn and sun-warmed pool. Soft rains left the world with the clean scent of flowers planted by his volunteer gardener. Pete Newman, college graduate, became Peter Newman, respected business man and community member, and he walked like a man who knows where he is going.

Without being consciously aware of such changes, his business instinct stepped in as a mental guide. For every problem solved, there came others demanding their fair share of attention. So far, he had handled all of them.

Remembering his awkwardness when showing Kelly Richardson the apartment she now occupied, he thought perhaps he had mishandled some of them, but now all but five of the apartments were occupied. His bank balance fed his confidence and subdued his apprehension. Former fears receded to the back burner of his brain. Peter Newman, the apartment owner, was a viable member of his community.

"My feeling fluctuates with my bank account", he told Chary on a day that had produced harmony in his personal world. "I'm exuding wealth at this moment. Would you care to share a bit of it and have a cup of coffee with me?"

"Oh, MAN! That's very generous of you. I will take you up on that if you think you can afford it. What brand are we having today?" Chary gave his head a half shake and laughed.

"As a matter of fact, it is Cuban. Strong, full flavored and freshly made. Would that appeal to your taste buds, Sir?" Pete put on the face that his sister used to call his hurting expression. "Or does your southern yen demand beer?"

"You know something, Pete? I'm glad I moved in here. You are beginning to feel like a brother to me, and I like that. Coffee will serve quite well, don't you think?"

"It's your call, man." Pete felt warm inside as though they really were brothers.

Soon thereafter, when an invitation was delivered to his mailbox, Pete was a bit surprised. A pool party? On Saturday afternoon next? Hosted by Kelly Richardson? And she was inviting ALL the residents to attend? Even Mrs. Strickland and Frank Fisher? Something about this mixture did not produce a smooth feeling. Was there anything in their leases that prohibited it?

Pete pulled out one of the blank lease forms and ran his finger over every line as he considered the possibility of a misused phrase. There was nothing. Should there have been a clause to protect the privacy and quiet of the tenants like Mrs.

S? Well, there was nothing he could do about it now. Maybe it might be good to get everyone acquainted. Interesting at any rate. He dialed Kelly's telephone, voiced his approval and thanked her for inviting him. He wondered if she was aware that her voice was so seductive. "Probably so," he decided with her voice still echoing in his head.

His first thought was to see that the grounds were flawlessly clean and neatly trimmed. Frank's phone was not answered on the first two or three rings. No sooner than he hung up his receiver than it rang. Frank was just out of the shower.

"Frank, have you received your party invitation yet?"

"Yes. Isn't it a lovely gesture? I was thinking I must see that everything is tidy. What do you think?"

"Good idea. You do not mind doing it?"

"Certainly not! I take it as my responsibility. How many tenants are there now? Do you think they will all attend?" Frank's enthusiasm was contagious.

"We have only three units unfilled, and most of those are single occupants. I am guessing we have about eighty people altogether. Probably half of those will show up for the party. My dad always said the tenants expected quiet surroundings; so he wouldn't have had a noisy party going on."I really appreciate your help in seeing that the grass is mowed, and the bushes are trimmed. I know Ms. Richardson will appreciate it, too. You might ask her what we can do to help make a success of her party?"

As it turned out, Kelly Richardson needed no help with her festive plans. Saturday morning dawned with the expectation of sunshine. The courtyard, already dressed with dozens of brilliant balloons, greeted early risers and promised to do the same for late sleepers. By noon the stereo system was in operation. Promptly at eleven thirty the hostess appeared in a swimsuit designed to detract from any possible physical flaw. If the brilliant colors did not support that aim, the cut of the cloth did.

Frank Fisher, coming from the second floor, stopped midway on the stairs and gaped.

"I didn't know her legs were that long", he muttered to no one in particular.

"Good afternoon, Mr. Fisher. I was hoping you would be here so I could tell you how chummy you have made everything look. I saw you making things ready, and I just want you to know how much it means to me. It is going to be a wonderful party, don't you think?"

"Indeed I do, Miss Richardson. Indeed I do". Frank continued to descend the stairs, his attempt to walk taller calling attention to his deliberately taut stomach muscles.

Like actors waiting in the wings for their cues, they arrived, the fat and the thin, the entree and the desserts. Within minutes chatter and unchecked laughter muted the stereo music. The party came alive.

Very few saw the caterers spreading the long table with picnic foods, but none missed the color scheme used in the food selection. The balloons repeated the rainbow of colors. Most persons were noticing that Kelly's swimsuit and see-through cover-up also matched. The men were more conscious of the glimmer of the thin gold chain delicately caressing her ankle. Kelly appeared oblivious to the whistles and banter. Clearly, her efforts were producing the desired results.

She had thought of everything, including the timing of events. Before the caterers left, they produced stacks of generous and thirsty towels that acknowledged the happy color scheme. The Hostess made a perfect dive into the pool. Neither splash nor ripple marred her under-water swim from end to end of the pool. She turned and returned to the corner steps. Moving with practiced showmanship, she exited, displaying her shapely body to its best advantage. One of the towel bearers draped her. Another signaled for the others to follow her lead. Nothing more was needed. In a flash, the food and drink tables were crowded areas and the pool a sea of bobbing heads. An hour later, as the pace slowed, Kelly again claimed attention.

"It is time we get acquainted. It's no fun to have all this fun and not know the people we are sharing it with. We have a perfect game for it, too. I will go around the pool and let you tell your NAME and anything else you want to tell. We have magic beans to assist you. If you cannot remember who you are, you may have a red "Memory bean." She held up a red bean she took from a filled basket. "And, if you talk too long, you may have a green mileage bean. The purple ones go to the shy people. They may signal Pete to speak for them if they are too timid to do it for themselves. Everyone else earns a white jellybean just for calling out your name and waving; so we will all know you. Who wants to be first? No one? Very well. I will be first.

"My name is Kelly Richardson. I am a hostess at the Colonial Country Club. I am old enough to know better, and I want all of you to meet my boss, Manny La Banta. It was he who furnished this yummy food and the party favors. He doesn't want to speak, but he won't be insulted if you thank him for your pretty towel. Now, who's next?"

"You talked too long, Kelly. Take your Mileage Pill." Frank prompted.

"Thank you, for reminding me." She took a bean from the basket of miniature Easter Eggs and swallowed it. Then, she pushed the basket toward Frank. "And who are you, sir?" Frank Fisher, Madam. I am the in-house gardener here, and I must complain that your colorful decorations are putting my plants to shame." "No they are NOT!" came the sound of combined voices.

Kelly bowed in mock gratitude to the group and continued her round with the bean basket. Manny declined the opportunity to speak, and she continued to hand a bean to each party guest. She made her way to where The Three Peas were sitting on a blanket. Patti and Pris were obstreperous in their chance to be spotlighted. Paula, to the contrary, wanted to say something, but seemed too shy to do so.

"Was there something else you wanted to say, Paula?" Kelly asked.

"Well, I was just wishing I could swim like you do."

"Let's work on that together, shall we? I'll be happy to help you."

"You will? Oh, that's just great, Kelly. That really is!" Paula sat down again.

"Maybe you should take a Remembering pill so you won't forget that promise." Chary bantered.

"I will." Kelly laughed and took another bean. "Why don't we hear from Peter Newman." She beckoned Pete to join her.

"They all know me." Pete attempted to decline the invitation.

"Well, maybe you don't know yourself. We'll just have to give you a knowledge pill. Don't we have one of those, Manny?"

"There are some of those in there, too."

She handed a yellow jellybean to Pete. Left with no choice, Pete took a jellybean and swallowed it.

"I am Pete, the man who gets blamed when anything goes wrong around here," he offered and reattached himself to his seat.

Kelly threw him a kiss and continued. Seeing Chary, she invited: "You and Pete seem to be quite close. Why don't you tell us about yourself as well as whatever you care to say about him." Scanning the basket contents, she came up with a yellow pill and laid it in Chary's hand, her own wrist and delicate fingers seductively turned for maximum effect.

"That looks like the last of the knowledge pills, Chary, so tell us who you are."

"Aw, Man!" Chary uttered, as he swallowed the jellybean. "I am Charles Reasoner, but I answer to 'Chary'. Pete and I are close only because we reside next to each other. He is my Landlord, and I wouldn't want to upset him by telling on him. Seriously, though, I think he is a great guy." Chary looked around him and shrugged his shoulders as he sat.

Seeing one of the guests preparing to depart, Kelly accelerated the pace of the game. Pushing the basket into his reach, she entreated him. "Come on. Tell us who you are and where are you employed?"

"My name is Gene Seals, and I'm a automobile mechanic. Pete is one of my customers, or am I allowed to say that?"

"That admission is saying a lot, Gene. Where is your business, and can you accommodate one more customer?" Kelly held the mike under Gene's mouth.

"I run that shop two blocks north of that church down the street, and I'd be glad to have anybody in this group to stop by any time, WITH OR WITHOUT A PROBLEM."

This speech produced hearty laughter, and Kelly handed the basket to Frank.

“Frank, will you please pass the basket around and let everyone take one and get on with the introductions before Gene lures everybody to his place tonight.” Okay?” Kelly smiled at Frank as he strode to her side to accept the basket.

“Beware of Greeks bearing gifts” Chary called and chuckled.

The couple from number forty looked at each other and shrugged. A few stood up to leave, claiming early Sunday engagements, but Frank reached them and urged them to take a jellybean before they left. In friendly good humor they complied. Neighborhood unity was solidified, and the hostess was pleased.

Mrs. Strickland almost reached number twenty before Frank caught her and insisted that she have a jellybean and her towel. She pushed both aside and continued toward her apartment. Seeing the dejection on his face, she offered:

“Don’t mind me. I’m just a cranky old woman with Arthritis and indigestion. Maybe I am a little bit jealous of our hostess because I can not wear a bathing suit like that. I don’t know. When you become my age, you won’t know why you act the way you do, either. You are all right, though, Frank. You are doing a fine job of keeping this place clean. You’ve been needed around here for a long time, and I hope you stay around as long as I am here.” She turned to continue toward her apartment.

“Aw, come on, Mrs. Strickland. Be a good sport and take a jellybean. Miss Richardson went to a lot of trouble and expense so we could all get acquainted. Just let them see what a good sport you are.” He pushed the basket toward her.

“Well, all right, then.” She picked one and held it up for the revelers to see her swallow it. The applause was instant and hearty. Laughter was spreading. Joviality increased among the remaining guests.

Manny nodded to Frank, waved a goodnight to the guests and kissed Kelly on the cheek. She followed him to his car as Frank continued to make the round of remaining guests. He offered the basket to each and insisted that they join in the spirit of the evening.

Kelly’s absence was noticeable in the quieter mood of the remaining guests. A few more opted to call it a night.

Pete was staring toward the entrance that had swallowed all sight of Kelly Richardson.

“She should not have followed LaBanta!,” he muttered. The thought of her being with Manny Labanta produced an unfamiliar and inner storm. Suddenly he eased back into his lounge chair and became quiet. The veins of his hands dictated an agitated dance.

Half rising from the folding chair on which he sat, his head turned toward the front of the building that was hiding the departing couple.

Chapter III

Quite unexpected are the woes
Infiltering our gay times,
When executed by known foes
Who are messing with our minds
pkh

"What's the matter, Pete?" Chary sat in the chair near his landlord. "Are you okay?"

"I feel like somebody else."

"Who do you feel like, Pete?"

"I don't know; maybe like YOU."

Chary frowned and thought about that possibility.

"I guess that might be all right. You can be me, and I will be you. Will that work?"

" NO. You are a right brain, and I am a left brain".

"That's right, I couldn't handle your job. Maybe we can just be the same person then. Can we do that?"

"Sure. We can do that, but will we be Pete or Chary?" Pete had not forgotten about his concern of Kelly with LaBanta. "I don't want to be Manny", he grumbled.

" Maybe we could be one person with two names. What name do you want?

"I want to be William, and be called Bill. How about you?"

I will be Robert, and you can call me Bob. We will be Billy-Bob. How's that?"

"That is perfect, Bob. I feel better after getting that settled, don't you?"

" Absolutely! Aren't we ready to call it a night, Bill?"

"Absolutely!"

They disappeared arm in arm, and nothing more was seen of Billy Bob that evening. No one seemed to notice or to care.

One after another the participants gathered towels and the left-over sandwiches for the long journey home. Laughter grew fainter as each located the correct door to fit the key he carried. Kelly reappeared and offered to assist Paula with her swimming technique. By eleven o'clock the only sound to be heard was the ripple of water responding to the circulating pump. In the Manager's unit, two men lay sprawled across one bed, fully dressed and neither knowing nor caring. Sunday morning would come and depart before anyone awoke. Nothing lingered from the party except the gurgling water and the faint smell of chlorine, hamburger and suntan lotion.

Pete opened his eyes and realized the day was well advanced. He had not slept this soundly for longer than he could remember. Nor could he remember when he had EVER dreamed such vivid dreams. Sensing another person in the room with him, he jerked himself upright. It was merely Chary, he thought. In another minute he jolted upright, fully awake. *"Chary, wh-wh-what- what are you d-d-doing in here?"*

"Billy, it is Bob. Don't you know me?"

"N-no. Yuh-yuh-yuh're n-not Bbbob. Yuh-yuh're Ch-Ch-Chary"

Chary shook his head to clear it. He squinted at Pete through narrowed eyelids.Wh-wh-what's going on?" He continued to be confused.

"I th-th-think w-w-we got dr-dr-unk last night" Chary shook his head once more. He tried to stand, but the floor was moving like a surf board fighting angry waves. Finally he stooped and crawled to the door. Pete crawled over to help him open the door. With this accomplished, Chary crawled out to the sidewalk and on to his unit next door, fumbling for his key which seemed to have been lost in the swimming pool. Having no other choice, he sagged against the door and went back to sleep until later that Sunday afternoon.

Pete stumbled into the bathroom. The shower cleared his head somewhat, but his memory of the past evening was as vague as the answers to questions spinning in his mind.. He recalled the Get-Acquainted Party, and wondered why no one else appeared as affected as he did. Or did they? Did everyone have sandwiches to eat? Could they have been a bit bad? Worse still, were any of the tenants ill, and how about Mrs. Strickland. Was she okay? Suddenly, it was important to make a check of everyone.

Mrs. Strickland's telephone was not answered when he called. He dialed other numbers of the couples who had been there. Most were groggy from sleeping so late but were well. Only Kevin and Jane Keystone admitted feeling slightly ill this morning. She was pregnant, though; so that didn't count.

They were having breakfast, Kevin said. Yes, they had slept well. It was a great party. No, they did not have a touch of food poisoning. They were sorry they had left before the games started, though. They had been tired and wanted to get to bed early.

"I do hope we did not disrupt the fun by leaving."

"Oh, not at all. Not at all." Pete was emphatic. "Glad you enjoyed it."

So it was not the food. He mused. Then what? He decided to knock on Mrs. Strickland's door. After the third knock, she opened it.

"Are you all right this morning, Mrs. Strickland? I hope the party was not too disturbing for you."

"Well, no, Mr. Newman, it didn't bother me a bit. In fact I rather enjoyed it after I came inside. It did do me good to listen to all those young people laughing. I found myself remembering my own younger days, and I played some of my old records and danced all by myself. I did over-sleep this morning, though; so I didn't go to church as I usually do.

June is a perfect time for a get together, don't you think?"

"I guess we all let our hair down a bit, didn't we? I just wanted to know that you weren't disturbed. You are right. June is a great time for a party Have a good day, Mrs. Strickland".

"You do the same, Mr. Newman."

Imagine old Mrs. S up here dancing to her favorite old tunes! He'd have enjoyed seeing that. Pete's left-brain thinking took over. No one complained of any harm or illness. It was not food poisoning. Everyone, including himself, admitted to having had a restful sleep, and no one was disturbed by the gaiety. So what was he worried about? He would simply let it be. Later he would call Frank Fisher to express his appreciation for the tidy grounds. After all, it was Frank who assumed the chore of clearing the party debris after everyone else had retired. He continued to Chary's apartment and raised his hand to knock just as the door opened. Chary was dressed and smelling of good bath soap.

"Good Morning, Neighbor. Are you in one piece after the wing-ding yesterday?" Pete watched for any unusual reaction to the question..

"Pete, I feel great now, but I was coming over to talk to you about the dream I had. Do you have time to listen to an outlandish story?"

"Certainly. Come on over to my place right now, if you like. I'll make coffee."

"None for me, thanks. Pete, this was the strangest dream I ever had. It seemed real, if you know what I mean. Like it was really happening."

"I think I know what you mean, Chary. Tell me about your dream. What happened?"

Like boiling water bubbling over the edge of a pot, Charles Reasoner could not wait until they reached Pete's place. He began to relate the details of the dream even as they walked.

"Well, you and I were twin brothers, and we lived with our parents in a tiny little town some place that was very cold. We had to get warm around an old wood -burning stove, and our mom kept calling us to get up and get dressed for Sunday School. She was frying eggs and ham, and she had made biscuits in a funny looking black stove. There was a teakettle of boiling water setting on the back of it. She poured some water in a pan, and our dad used it to wash his face and hands."

"Go on. What happened?" Pete had forgotten about coffee. This was unbelievable!

"Well, she called me 'Bobby', and told me to go get you out of bed...only she called you 'Billy', and it was really you, Pete. You looked just like you do right now, and our dad said to hurry so we wouldn't be late."

" Okay, Okay. What then?" Pete had to remind himself to breathe.

"WELL, YOU CAME IN AND TOLD DAD YOU WERE TOO BIG TO BE GOING TO SUNDAY SCHOOL, and.."

"And WHAT? COME ON, Chary. What else did Billy say?"

"You didn't have time to say anything further. Dad threw a right and knocked you flat. Mom rushed over to see about your bloody nose, but dad told her to leave you alone.

Then he said to you, 'TAKE HEED WHEN YOU STAND LEST YOU FALL, BILLY. NOW GET DRESSED FOR SUNDAY SCHOOL AND DON'T GET BLOOD ALL OVER YOUR CLOTHES!"

Chary swallowed and sat back in his chair and put a trembling hand to his forehead.

"What do you make of that, Pete? It all seemed too real to be a dream."

"Chary, You're not going to believe this, but I HAD THAT SAME DREAM. It was in the same house with those same parents, and we had the same names, and our dad knocked me down for not respecting the FIRST COMMANDMENT. WHILE YOU WERE TELLING YOUR DREAM, I COULD ALMOST HEAR DAD YELLING THOU SHALL HAVE NO OTHER GODS BEFORE ME."

"And we looked just like we do right now, but I don't know how we could look the same as we do now. We're from different parents, aren't we?"

Pete was trembling. He looked at Chary who was sobbing and trying to continue his story.

"But HOW could this happen, Pete? It's almost like we were carried to another land. It is frightening, Pete, and that's not all that happened."

"What else, Chary? I think I know what you are going to say, though. You were so scared and protective of me that .."

"I looked around for something to hit dad with. I was so mad at him that I grabbed his straight edge razor and slashed his face, just missing his eyes." Chary's cries became a flood of remorse and shame. He crouched and hugged himself into a sobbing bundle of dejection.

Pete knelt and laid his hand on the distraught man's shoulder.

"How could it just be a dream, Pete? Were we both drugged?"

"THAT'S IT! Chary. Could we have been tripping without realizing it? I think we can safely say that, but let's learn more about it first. Okay?"

"I agree with you, Pete., but HOW?"

For one thing, let's find out more about those jelly beans, what was in them, where they came from and what damage can they do to us."

"Will I be in trouble, Pete?"

Pete's logical thinking recognized genuine terror in the voice. Clapping Chary on the shoulder, he attempted to release the hold fear had on the other man.

"It was a dream, Chary. It didn't happen. We're not even the same race. How could we have the same parents? We never even met until you came here to rent an apartment. Our dreams just got mingled together, that's all. Drugs can drive a man crazy; we both know that."

"Sure! I am half Latino, and you are an Anglo, and we never saw each other before a couple of months ago when I rented my apartment. Nothing's really changed, is it?" Chary was reaching for a sane explanation."Right. Our dreams were just that...DREAMS!."

As usual, when faced with a problem, Pete's reasoning led him into and out of a maze of possibilities. Drugs? Certainly! Jelly Beans? Undoubtedly! Furnished by Kelly Richardson? Probably. Planned by Manny La Banta? Without a doubt! Why? For what purpose? No answer came forth. Were there any left?

This question jarred Pete. Who would have them? Frank, of course. But why? Would he have picked them up as a general cleanup of the area? If so, would he still have them? Did he intend to give them back to Kelly? Did he plan on using them for his own pleasure? Were they addictive? Who would have the answers to his questions? In fact, he needed to know if any were left after having been passed around.WHAT SHOULD HE DO NOW? He looked at Chary curled in fetal position and bemoaning his detestable past.

"Come on, Chary! That stuff is potent mental stimulus. Stop thinking of it as your own story. I think the game about our names that we played last night caused us to dream a related episode. Go home and play tidily winks on your computer, or whatever you do as a computer analyst. I have a big day today, and I need to get started. I'll see you later. Okay?"

Chary's eyes fell to the floor, but he edged his way to the door and on to the next unit.Pete was half way up the stairs toward Frank's apartment by the time Chary closed his door. Anyone who thought running an apartment complex was a trouble free method of survival was in need of help. He hoped he could withstand whatever came next.

Frank did not answer his knock. Pete frowned before deciding the situation called for unorthodox attention. Glancing around to see who might be in the courtyard and seeing no one, he put his master key in the lock and opened the door. He left the door ajar and entered quickly to scan the obvious areas. On the coffee table was the basket half full of multi-colored jellybeans laying next to three different cameras. The guy must really be a camera buff, he thought. Feeling like a felon, Pete scooped up a handful of the beans and dropped them into his pocket. He turned to leave just as Frank Fisher entered. The two men gazed at each other for seconds before either spoke.

"Oh, hello, Frank! You didn't answer when I knocked; so I thought I should check on you. You are all right I see. I just wanted to make sure none of our tenants had any problems from last night's party. It is the first time we've ever done anything like that. But, as I see, YOU ARE IN TOP SHAPE." Pete took a couple of steps toward the door.

"No, I had no problem. Why? Did something happen to someone else?" *Was there suspicion lurking under Frank's question?*

"Everyone, including Mrs. Strickland, seems to be in top shape. In fact, some may even have slept better than they have in months. How about you?"

"I did not notice anything different from my normal sleep, but I thank you for your concern. May I offer you coffee?"

"Thanks. Another time? But I do want to thank you for cleaning up after the party last night. You have made this place a much nicer place, Frank."

"Thank you, Pete. I appreciate knowing my efforts are making a difference. Being free to do a bit of gardening is a real pleasure for me."

"Well, I'll get on with checking on everyone."

Pete wished he could think of a better ending to this conversation. On his way down the stairs, he took one long, slow breath and blew it out through puffed cheeks.

"Whew!"

He was not cut out for cloak and dagger activities. Yet, on the other hand, he must see the investigation through to the end. There were SO MANY QUESTIONS! First, he needed to know WHAT HAD HAPPENED? Then WHY? But right now the biggie was WHAT SHOULD HE DO NEXT?

What he had in his pocket was definitely NOT a pocket full of sunshine.

Now that he had them, where could he go to find out about them? A pharmacy?

Not the Police, There was nothing to be gained by courting trouble for the place. He discarded most of the ideas which rolled through his mind. He reconsidered the first idea. He would get to a pharmacist at once. Then what? Right this minute he would enjoy punching that Manny LaBanta in the nose What right had he to be here at a get acquainted pool party for the tenants? Pete noticed he was clenching his fists. Moreover, he recognized the silver taste of fear in the back of his throat.

He relaxed his hands. Right now he should be getting to the bottom of the mess.

Pulling the keys from his pocket brought one of the beans out to bounce like an accusing finger as it rolled under a plant. His knees complained a bit in kneeling to retrieve it. His hasty glance to see whether anyone had seen the stealthy movement left him breathless. He had not indulged in games of this sort when he was a child. Certainly he would have preferred to forego them now.

Having retrieved the elusive jelly bean, his next move was a positive direction toward his own unit. Inside, he closed and locked the door and leaned against it to savor the feeling of safety from prying eyes. It would take a few minutes to unwind the tension wires that were wound around his lungs. Breathing had never been so difficult.

Fully an hour later, he gave a grateful sigh of relief. Although there had been no dangerous encounter during the frightening action he had instigated, he could almost feel himself promising whatever powers there were that he would not repeat such activity.

The pharmacist would be able to tell him what is in these little jellybeans and also how much harm they could do. Tomorrow morning would be dedicated to finding some answers. Meanwhile, he would ask Chary to spend the day with him. Perhaps company would dispel Chary's fears.

There was something more he must do before inviting Chary, though. He went directly to the small kitchen and opened a drawer. There he found a plastic sandwich bag. Carefully he reached into his pocket to extricate those worrisome jellybeans and to secure them. Only then did he dare to think about the last few minutes and what they might have been like had they been witnessed. What if Frank had asked to see what was in his pocket? More important at this juncture was secreting the evidence. Where should he stash them until the next morning? First one location, then another, was ruled out. The 'key board', of course. No one would think to search for jellybeans hanging from a peg like all the other 'keys'. He smiled at the meaningful symbol as he secured the bag to an unused key peg. No one would bother the candies there. The thought reminded him of an old high school English assignment to read 'The Purloined Letter'.

Shaking his head at this unaccustomed feeling of guilt, Pete threw back his shoulders, closed the door to the keyboard closet and headed for Chary's place. There was no answer to his knocks. He paused for a bit before deciding, for the second time today, that this was an emergency dictating the use of the Master key. He found Chary huddled in a corner of the tapestry sofa. The darkening sky was lighted moments at a time by fiery flashes of lightening, and the rumble of thunder climaxed the announcement with a prophetic roar.

For the next several hours Pete's attention was fixed on Chary; in cajoling and reasoning with him. It was more important NOW than it had earlier been. No longer could he accept the idea that such confrontation was an accidental event. There might be no doubt that the past still existed, but, even if it did, his main interest at this point was WHO and WHY had the event been an attraction to such a well planned pool party? WHAT COULD POSSIBLY BE ANYONE'S MOTIVE FOR PUTTING OTHERS THROUGH AN EXPERIENCE SUCH AS THIS? If it was a deliberate act of controlling another's mind, WHY?

Are human actions stored in some unimaginable disc ready for replay at the most propitious opportunity? Could mental telepathy cause dreams to merge between persons?

Monday morning ushered the rain that threatened to cancel his trip to the pharmacy. Pete reached into the end of the closet for his yellow raincoat, the one with the large pockets that could camouflage a bulky sandwich bag. Usually he hated the yellow hat that was part of the set; it made him look like a fire fighter, and he did not like extinguishing fires. Today was different. The first fire was at the pharmacy, and he left at once.Peter Newman knew that driving on Dallas streets the first few minutes of a rain could be extremely dangerous when one was required to use his brakes. The streets, glazed with the oily scum of daily traffic, required great caution, but Pete's mind was on the urgency of his mission. It was only his watchfulness that allowed him to maneuver around a two-car fender bender thus preventing his own mishap. He took a deep breath and exhaled slowly as he passed.

He took the first available parking space although it was a half block from his destination. As he walked to the entrance, a car backed from the parking space at the front door of the pharmacy. He gave himself a mental kick. He had believed in his 'Front Door Parking" rule for enough years to realize he could always depend on it if he simply thought about it; yet here he was on a rainy day grabbing like a desperate man at the first parking spot he saw! His mood was not improved when the car backed out of the space directly in front of the pharmacy door.

Stomping the water from his feet, he entered and turned toward the drug department. Fortunately there was no line waiting for service. May I help you?

"I'd like to speak to the pharmacist, please".

"I AM THE PHARMACIST."

"Sorry, I, uh, you uh...." This was not going well at all.

"You think I look too young. Right? Try me. I may surprise you."

"Well, a friend of mine has this teen age boy, you see. And he found some candies he thinks may be drugs in the kid's room. Can you tell me about them?" He opened the bag to display his find.

"Sir, I can tell you without testing that those 'candies' contain enough dextromethorphan to send a party of thirty on a trip they may wish they had not taken. They contain the same ingredients used in dozens of cough suppressing medications the kids are using today. Candies like those are used like any other cough depressant. We sell them right here, over the counter. No prescription required. It's that easy!"

"Then it is not a controlled substance. Right?"

"As I said, we sell them without a prescription. No, they are not controlled. Are they dangerous? If becoming addicted to a mind altering substance is dangerous, then, YES, THEY ARE DANGEROUS. And they are sold right over the counter.

"And kids are buying them*?"* Pete stood looking at the pharmacist in utter disbelief.

"Legally? Are you telling me this addictive substance is legal?

"It's not only legal, but there is no age limit required to buy it. I don't like it, either, but my hands are tied"

"What can be done to stop it?"

"Tell your friend he had better have plenty of money before he attempts to challenge large pharmaceutical companies, and he'd better have a few Senators in his coat pocket, as well. If the whole country can't prevent the tobacco companies from selling cancer inducing products, do you think it will be a snap to put the lid on cough syrups and pills? And before it is over, your friend will be forced to challenge the big publishers that make money on the ads for these leaches. You ask me what can be done about it. I'm telling you that is the way this slimy game is played, and it may already be too late to save this generation of kids. But, hey, what do I know? I am just a young pharmacist working on a salary and trying to make enough to pay off the tuition for his training. Can I do anything else for you today?"

"No. I think you answered all my questions. Thank you." Pete was stunned. by this encounter with truth. He returned the jellybeans to his pocket and turned to leave. For once, he was not tempted to browse among the shelves on his way out.

The rain was coming in torrents now, forcing Pete to lower his head to dive into it on his way toward his car. As he opened the car door, he fought with the gust as he tugged the door closed.

"Ooh Man!" He started the engine and eased back into the lane so water bound that it was difficult to make out the shapes of curbs. His mind was the busiest it had ever been. Where had he been the past several years while these things were going on? Why hadn't someone curbed the momentum? How widespread was it? What could he do about it? What could anybody do? Didn't anybody care? He turned at the corner leading to the apartment, but his mind was so occupied that he drove past the familiar building without realizing it.

"It's like the story of Adam and the apple in the Garden of Eden", he said aloud. 'MAYBE THIS IS THE SAME THING, NOT JUST LIKE IT." Pete slammed on the brakes to avoid hitting a kid on a bicycle Was that kid familiar with the jellybeans, he wondered. Did the kid have a dream about his past life? Was everybody here to undo his past mistakes? HE WISHED HIS DAD WERE ALIVE TO TALK ABOUT THESE THINGS. Would his dad have known of them? Which dad? The one in this lifetime, or the one in his dream? Were there others? What was reality here?

The kaleidoscope of questions continued through his head like a spate of rain water rushing the sloping road gutters. He pulled into a driveway and backed out to turn around and drive back to the apartments. He parked his car in its customary place and sat for a while wrestling with racing thoughts.

He had to talk to someone about this whole affair. It was just too big, and frightening and unbelievable to be pushed into a corner of his mind and left. The only people he could think of who might have some answers were preachers, and he was so out of touch with any church that he didn't know where to begin. And what about Chary? That poor guy is a basket case.

Thinking thus, Pete took the keys out of the ignition and flung open the wide door of the metallic gray BMW. He locked the car door and almost ran to his apartment. The telephone was ringing as he opened the door. It was Mrs. Strickland. Pete let out a sigh.

Why did that thing have to go off every time he needed undisturbed moments for sorting out his thoughts? And why did it always have to be Mrs. Strickland calling?

"What can I do for you, Mrs. Strickland?"

"Mr. Newman, what in the world is going on in apartment thirty three? That girl screamed and screamed for a long time before the police came. Has there been an accident or something?"

Pete closed his eyes for an instant before answering her.

"I'll get right on it, Mrs. Strickland. I don't know anything about it because I just came in. My telephone was ringing as I opened the door. Excuse me. I'll go right up."

He took the stairs two at a time and was relieved to see Frank standing near the door of number thirty three, looking as though he was studying the garden below.

"What is it, Frank?"

"Somebody roughed Paula up, I think, but I can't get much out of the other girls. I The cops took her downtown. I don't think she is hurt, but I do know those girls have been doing an awful lot of entertaining since they moved in here."

Chapter IV

When the fight begins within himself,
A man's worth something.
Bishop Blougram

"YOU DON'T MEAN WHAT I THINK YOU MEAN, DO YOU?"

"Pete, why do you think those women took three separate apartments instead of doing the room-mate bit and sharing rents? Surely you have noticed the various men who visit them. You HAVE TO HAVE BEEN AWARE THAT THEY ARE ENTERTAINING. I know you're not that naive. I even have a picture of one of the men paying one of the girls. Of course, I had no idea at the time what the payment was for, but cameras don't lie, Pete." Frank excused himself and made his way down the steps to his garden duties, seemingly unaware of the pelting rain.

Pete's heart was beating too fast. He knew it. Swallowing did not alleviate the pace. Nor did the rain let up. Here was that fast paced heart rate that threatened him whenever circumstances overwhelmed him. He tried to rationalize this latest event. He had refused to believe what his intuition dictated to him when these three women moved in. OF COURSE THEY WERE PROSTITUTES, AND NOW HE WAS BEING forced to admit it. NOW. It could not be thought about later. NOW HE WAS DEFINITELY INVOLVED, like it or not.

He knocked on the door of number thirty-three and waited in a whirlpool of disbelief until Patti opened it very slightly. Her hair was wrapped in a towel, and her terry cloth robe announced her annoyance at being disturbed from her bath. Right this minute Pete could not be put off by her camouflage. When Patti started to close the door, his foot was faster.

"Please don't do that, Patti. I have to know what is going on, and I have to know NOW." Having spoken, he nudged the door fully open. Two men in their early twenties were sitting inside on the sofa. Pete backed up and looked at the apartment number above the door. Number thirty-three. Paula's apartment. Patti brushed against him as she stepped outside and closed the door.

"Don't get all shook up, Pete", she said. "Paula's date got a little rough with her, and I came over to lend a hand. These guys are cousins of mine who just came over to invite me to a family reunion. They came with me when I came to Paula's apartment. Pris came over, too, and I think she called 911. Then the police came. I'm so sorry for all the commotion, but everything is under control. Really, it is."

Pete's eyes narrowed as he studied the girl's face.

"So you are telling me that you were just washing your hair when your ...did you say 'cousins'...came to visit? Patti, that's the lamest excuse I have ever heard. It is not only unconvincing. It is downright laughable, except that I'd much rather cry."As his voice rose, the two men stepped outside, one on either side of Patti.

"Maybe we ought to get going, Patti?" It was a question rather than a statement.

"OK, I'm sure everything is going to be all right. Isn't it, Pete?"

Pete Newman was certain of but one thing at this moment. He had one huge mess on his hands, and he hadn't a clue as to how to handle it. He watched the two men going down the steps and was aware that they had to walk around Frank and the water hose he was arranging near the pool. Patti waited for Pete's indication that she was free to go to her own unit. Her innocent pose and helplessness did not alleviate the gnawing in his middle, nor did they belie his suspicions.

"We'll talk later, Patti." On his way down the stairs, Pete realized the jellybeans were in his pocket. He would have dodged Frank Fisher had it been possible, but Frank stopped him.

"Pete, I happened to get a picture of those two guys and their car in case you need it."

"Good for you. I don't think we will need a picture, but you never can tell, can you?"

"That's right. You never know. I will keep them for you, anyway. How is your next door neighbor getting long? He seemed quite distressed about you on Saturday evening. Even yesterday he looked like a man who was having trouble reaching the next rung on the ladder, if you know what I mean"

"I DO know what you mean, Frank. I think our friend may have been working too many hours lately. He may be feeling the weight of too many hours at the computer."

"Perhaps he should take a vacation, then. Does he get regular vacations from his company?"

"I have not the least idea. He has not discussed his working routine with me. But, right now I need to get out of these wet things."

"Hey, don't get touchy. I was not trying to pry. If it appeared that I was, I apologize. I need to be tending to some of my own business. I'll see you later." Frank turned his attention to the gardening matters and drifted away. Pete felt an unanswered question lurking in the wings.

Chary was staring out the window of his unit as Pete approached. Seeing him there, Pete stopped when the door opened. Chary's normally tanned skin looked like chalk, and his eyes were puffy. Priority number one appeared to be his neighbor at this time.

"Hey, Buddy, come on over to my pad and let me get my breath so we can make some plans about things in general."

Chary followed him like an obedient child. Pete opened the door and Chary went directly to the sofa and collapsed onto it.

"First, let me make a quick trip to the bathroom." Pete's sentence was finished by the time he opened the bathroom door. Shedding his raincoat he felt the bulky envelope of jellybeans. He opened the top drawer of the sink cabinet and thrust them into a back corner. In seconds he was back in the living room where Chary sat waiting. One look told him that the man had not eaten, and, to Pete, eating eliminated many of life's problems.

"Why don't I scramble some eggs and fix some toast while we chat. Okay?" He did not wait for an answer before undertaking that mission.

"Did the police leave? I thought they had come for me."

"No, they did not come for you, Chary. They came because one of the girls upstairs called them to break up some kind of a problem with a guest. Here, eat this. I'm not the greatest cook in the world, but I come up with a winning piece of toast."

He pushed a plate toward Chary and sat down across the table for his share. It was obvious that the Saturday evening event dominated Chary's thoughts. Pete attempted a change of topic matter.

"That was a nice little shower we had we had, wasn't it? Care for more toast?"

"Do you want me to move, Pete?"

"Why would I want you to move? NO, I want you to stay right there in the apartment next to mine. If you are still thinking about those dreams, FORGET THEM. TODAY IS NO DIFFERENT THAN THE DAY BEFORE THE POOL PARTY. Turn it loose, Chary. Besides, I like having you as my neighbor."

"Thanks, Pete. I like living next to you, too. Are you sure you have some more of that toast?" Chary's feeble effort to restore his usual humor was a welcome relief.

"Ooh, Man", Pete responded in kind. "It is a good thing I am such a great chef. Otherwise you would have to search the area for a comparable meal."

With breakfast finished and Chary's troubled appearance partially restored to normal, Pete pursued graver matters. His usual method was to list all that must be done to achieve a given goal. He began with problem number one: Tenants.

"How do you feel about all of our tenants, Chary? Any unusual personalities among them?"

"Well, certainly. Everyone that lives here is rather unique. Is that what you mean?"

"Not exactly. I'm trying to learn whether any of our people could be capable of drugging us?"

"Gosh, Pete. Are you thinking that maybe somebody here may have done so?"

"No. I don't even know what went on, and that's the question I have to ask first."

Seeing that Chary's anxiety was escalating, he changed the subject, but his mind stayed on track with its investigation.

"First, I must ascertain the depth of our problem. What went on? Who were all of the participants involved? How serious was the police record filed today? Was there a connection between the jellybeans and the police visit? What was the role of the two so called cousins with Patti in Paula's apartment? And if Frank was interested enough to have taken pictures, what was he looking for? What was his interest in this scenario? For another thing, how did Frank happen to be on hand on a working day? His increasing interest in the affairs of the other tenants is annoying. Come to think of it, didn't he have an awful lot of various cameras? Is it just natural curiosity, or is it more serious? Or am I becoming too suspicious about ordinary actions?" Pete suddenly realized he was asking these questions aloud and that Chary was sitting too still.

"Don't pay too much attention to my questioning mind, Chary. It's all a part of trying to stay on top of things. Care for more toast?""No, thanks, Pete. And I really do need to get back to my computer. I am trying to put together a course of study for one of the young men at our office. Thanks for the boost. I will see you later. Okay?" Chary moved like a man walking in his sleep.

"No problem." Pete went to the door with him, and, after locking the door behind himself, stepped outside to watch his neighbor enter his own unit. Seeing Frank trimming around the garden shrubs, he nodded approval of the improved appearance. Frank wiped his brow.

"Let's sit. The rain left the shrubs looking a little ragged; so I am trying to shape them a little bit." Frank pulled a cleaning cloth from his hip pocket and wiped the shears.

"I've been thinking about those pictures you took, Frank. I would like to see them."

"I thought you might after you got to thinking about them. I will get them for you."

"There is something else I wondered about, too, Frank. You are all right, aren't you? I mean, I notice you haven't been to work this week, and I wondered if something is wrong."

"No, I usually take Mondays off if we have a slow week at the office. The rain this morning gave me a perfect opportunity to stay in, and, then when it stopped, I decided to use the rest of the day touching things up. I really do enjoy gardening. I'm glad you have this area. My fondest dream is to own my own nursery some day. I'll run up and get those pictures for you."

Frank gathered his small pruning equipment and headed up the stairs. In minutes he was back, the pictures in hand. There was one of the two young men entering their car and one of the car's license plate. Pete's surprise showed on his face as he studied them. Frank explained. "I sometimes take pictures of action which might help me remember the occasion of the event covered. It seems to complete the picture. I had a feeling there ought to be a record of all of this when that girl started screaming the way she did," he said. "Keep these if like. I have copies. It is a hobby of mine to make copies of pictures I want to keep."

"Thank you. I don't know how these will help to solve anything, but you are right. It never hurts to have records of questionable activities. I wonder when Paula will be coming in and how this was handled downtown. In fact, I wonder if all of the events the past few days fit into one picture. It is baffling to say the least."

The two men sat without further talk, each aware of the unspoken questions floating between them.

"September will be here before we know it, won't it?"

"Right. Time is moving rapidly."

"True. And I can hardly believe I have been living here for six months. You have nice accommodations here, Pete. I know you are concerned about this morning's occurrence, but it is bound to happen now and then when this many people live this close together. You are doing a great job. If I can ever be of help to you, I hope you know you have it for the asking." Frank held his hand out to his landlord. His eyes sought Pete's and found them. Their hands met and held.

"I do appreciate that, Frank, and I may have to call on you sooner than I realize."

He called them 'nudges', these frequent Bible verses or the brief memories of past events that leaped into his mind at such appropriate places. With the feel of Frank's hand gripping his own, came a well remembered saying from another time. "BEFORE YE CALL I WILL ANSWER." He shuddered.

Could this be a 'nudge' to seek answers from some spiritual source? Was it an answer to the next item to be checked off his list? Was it MORE than that, perhaps? Could all of these uninvited nudges occur for a specific purpose? Were they pointers to a direction he should take? Could there be some magnetism, drawing together the oddly different personalities residing here? His cell phone interrupted his musing. Frank stood up and walked away as Pete answered it.

"Mr. Newman, could you come up for a few minutes? It is very important that I talk with you right away."

"Certainly, Mrs. Strickland, I will be right up."

The door to number twenty was standing open as he reached the top landing. Mrs. Strickland motioned toward a chair, and Pete sat, poised in readiness for her most recent upbraiding. He crossed his legs, and waited for her to begin. This was going to take some time, Pete thought. The old woman was obviously having a lot of trouble getting her story on the right track. He settled farther back to wait while she studied some notes she had made.

When, at last, Mrs. Strickland raised her eyes, Peter Newman became conscious of the ceaseless tears which tumbled down her face. Something was troubling her. He moved forward in his chair to help just as she gave a determined dab at her eyes and cleared her throat.

Chapter V

To renew ties with the past need not always be daydreaming;
It may be tapping old sources of strength for new tasks.
Simon Strunsk

"Mr. Newman, I owe you an apology." She waved away the denial appearing on his face. "Yes, I do. I have behaved badly toward you, and I am sorry. I am an old woman, and recently I have been feeling that my time is about up. I do not intend to leave this earth without rectifying the situation.

Uncomfortable, Pete shuffled his feet and shook his head, but she continued...

"What I am going to tell you will come as a shock, no doubt. Nonetheless, I must ask you to listen to the whole story before saying a single word. I have been watching those three girls living like LADIES OF THE NIGHT, and my first thought was that it served you right. I was even wrong in thinking such a low thought. For a long time I blamed your father for almost every unpleasant thing that ever happened to me. I never did forgive him for dying when he did, anyway." Mrs. Strickland gave another hand wave to brush his questions aside.

"You know I was hired to assist your father in running this place. I think I served him well because I was able to spot trouble before it ever materialized in many cases. We didn't have the types of predicaments you are experiencing. Believe me, I would have put a stop to that nonsense before it ever took roots if it had happened back then." He swallowed. A puzzled expression flickered over Pete's face. He leaned toward her to better understand this perplexing statement.

"Those three young women are openly practicing prostitution right here under our noses, and you haven't done a thing to prevent it. That one youngster is just a child. She is being used, and it seems to me it is your responsibility to see that it ends."

Pete's eyes flew wide open. Incredulity spread across his face. He started to speak, and nothing came from his lips. Again the lady stopped his interruption with a silencing signal from her hands.

"It may be too late to intervene on behalf of two of them, but I am certain the younger one could, and should, he guided out of that web. Right this minute, though, that is beside the point. Now that you are aware of the matter, I am sure you will take care of it. But back to the story I want to relate." She shifted her body to an easier position and brushed her skirt before folding her hands to continue.

"I knew your father many years ago; in fact, we were once engaged to be married, and we..." The phone in Pete's pocket interrupted her next words, startling both of them.

When Pete made no move to answer it, she shrugged her shoulders."Oh, go ahead and answer it," she ordered.

"Hello...WHAT? WHAT DID YOU SAY? WHERE? GET OUT RIGHT NOW!"Pete was on his feet in an instant, dialing 911.

"THE LAUNDRY ROOM IS ON FIRE!" he told her as he bolted out the door. He gave the address and directions to the designated location as he ran toward the units closest to the danger zone. Frank Fisher was already urging the tenants toward the front grounds as Pete bounded around the corner. He might have known the man would be doing what needed to be done. Sirens blared their way through the congregating mass. Pete's first thought was amazement at Frank's abilities. His next one was a moment of gratitude.

The fire engine screamed to a stop in the alley. Firemen flew from it as it stopped, each man sprinting to his assigned task. The isolated blaze was confined to the one area and quickly tapped out. Then came the concentrated inspection to determine the cause. It showed no irreparable damage, costly though it might be. Their advice was limited to having the laundry equipment owner install heavier wiring.

"And, of course you will want to inform your insurance company. They would likely pay for a paint job to rid the building of the grimy smoke." The fireman continued to check for further damage, pulling electric plugs to get to the backs of the washer and dryer.

He picked up an oily towel that might have been used to clean a lawn mower or other motor, sniffed it and dropped it into the trash receptacle.

"That's a bad habit to make," he uttered as it left his hands. "Do you do the lawn work here"?

"No. One of the tenants is also the grounds attendant. He volunteers just because he enjoys gardening, but I can't imagine him as a mechanic or mower cleaner. What do you think started this blaze?"

"There must have been a shortage in the dryer. It is that electric cord that shows damage. You're lucky we go here when we did. You could easily have had major damage to the apartments themselves. Count your blessings, man."

"I'm doing that right this minute, and that includes the Fire Department, Pete said."You guys got here almost before I did, and I was only upstairs. I certainly do appreciate your help."

"You know anything about those oily rags?"

"Not a thing. I have noticed some of the people living across the alley coming in and using the machines at times.

"Don't you keep this room locked when it is not being used?"

Pete wondered if the question held some sort of accusation."How in the world could I do that? Do you know how many people are using these machines DAY AND NIGHT?"

The fireman did not allow his gaze to stray from Pete's face. In a moment, he asked "Couldn't your renters have a key for this room?"

"Well, I hadn't thought of that! I'll do it! And, hey, I do thank all you guys for what you do. Seeing you work today didn't hurt my high opinion of you at all."The fireman laughed and quipped: "Good.! We will count on your help with our next drive for donations. Or would you rather take a couple of books of tickets to the next Fireman's Ball?"

"Try me for either one," Pete promised." The excitement was over. The tenants drifted back to their units, all except Mrs. Strickland who was watching from the upstairs walkway. Seeing Pete, she called down to him.

"Is everything under control?"

"The danger is over, but I need to get someone out here to install a lock for the laundry room and to make keys for everyone. We can finish our chat after that, if it's all right with you."

"Of course we can talk later, Mr. Newman. Is there anything I can do to help?"

"No, not right now, but I'll call you if I need you.

Pete muttered something to himself as his hand did an involuntary wave in her direction. She couldn't possibly know how tired he was at this moment. The odor of the fire and smoke performed a reeking afterplay which begged to be exterminated. That would be another requirement before he could get back to her.With the danger put to rest, and the firemen gone, Pete headed for his place. Hopefully he could get someone out today to do the key job.

Frank fell in step with him.

"Pete, have you ever considered joining the Apartment Association? That organization has a great deal of help for owners like yourself. For one thing, they keep a man near the capitol to keep updated on legal changes which might affect the industry. For another, they have copyrighted lease forms which only DESIRABLE tenants are willing to sign. Something like those might have prevented the problems you are dealing with from four apartments upstairs. I have the phone number if you would like to discuss membership with them." Frank, as usual, pitched an idea and left the fulfillment to the listener. He waited for an answer.Pete had heard his father speak of the meetings of the Apartment Owners Association, but he had never even wondered what they did or why it might be an integral part of his business. If his dad found it useful, perhaps he, too, should investigate it.

"Yes, I'd like to have the number, Frank, but I probably won't be able to call them until I get someone to secure the laundry room for us. But, YES, I would like to have that number."

He unlocked the office door and went directly to his desk. First things first. IF he could find the time to decide which thing was important enough to merit being first. He was relieved when Frank left him at the door.

As it turned out, luck was with him for a change. The locksmith would be out at once. Next, he would be able to let Mrs. Strickland get her message off her chest. He would listen to her story, whatever it was. How did this uncanny woman come up with such answers to such unasked questions? That might be the next 'first thing' to be laid to rest.

Wrong! Frank was back with the telephone number. Maybe....No.. Forget it. He would probably NEVER find another ten minutes to himself! Pete was one tired man. Frank's knuckles did a tap on the unlocked office door and followed the tap to give a slip of paper to Pete. He half waved and was out the door before Pete could voice his appreciation.

With his left hand cradling the receiver, his right hand dialed the number. His endurance was reaching for an end. Having heard Frank describe the benefits of the Rental Application Lease Contract Forms, he found it easy to see why undesirables such as occupied four of his units, would choose his place. THEY COULD NOT GET IN TO THOSE PROTECTED BY THE STRINGENT WORDING OF A PROPER LEASE AGREEMENT.

A person unwilling to answer these questions could be considered an undesirable. Right? Can they do that? Isn't that discrimination?" Pete was searching for a safe place to deposit his racing thoughts.

"Discriminating against WHAT?" He asked himself. ANY PROSPECTIVE TENANT CAN REFUSE TO SIGN THE FORM, AND HE CAN LOOK ELSEWHERE. If he DOES sign, he admits that he does not object to being investigated. He has nothing to hide and prefers to live in a protected complex that insures he will have quality neighbors. Look at the money to be saved in lawsuits, redecorating, advertising vacancies, checking references and chasing bad checks."

Pete re-read the leases signed by the three girls and two men in the upstairs units that were the trouble spots at this time. In view of the difference that one of the new leases might have made, he felt inadequate and stupid for not having noticed it earlier.

"I've led the vultures right to the chicken's nest. I should have been keeping a list of lessons I have learned in this business", he said to the pictures under the glass top of the desk. With something that could make this much difference in operating, it became important to get involved at once. Pete called the number which Frank had supplied. No answer. Seeing that Frank was still in the courtyard, he stepped outside to mention some of the things he had found.

"Frank, I was looking over the leases of former tenants and noticed the wording on the earliest ones were poorly chosen. For instance, there was one, which read 'NO BOTTLES ON THE PREMISES'. That is laughable. Not even a catsup bottle? How about a bottle of vinegar or milk? Can you imagine signing a legal document with such an order?

A person could be sued for having a bottle of iodine in the house. I can see why the rules have changed and why these new leases have come into being.

" I would never have guessed there could be so much protection in a few pieces of paper."

"Right! Back then you could have been sued for entering, uninvited, an apartment of a tenant, even if his rent was several weeks past due, and you had very little way to force him out. You may find many ways a membership assists you. By the way, have you heard from the girl the Police picked up?"

"Not a word, but it looks like I now have the opportunity. She is coming through the gate right this minute."

As Paula approached, Frank moved in the opposite direction. She started to pass Pete without speaking to him but changed her mind.

"I suppose you have a sermon for me, too, and you want me to move?"

"No, I do think you are making a big mistake in your choice of activities in life, but I do not want you to move. I do, however, think you should be more discriminating in your choice of company. In fact, for the benefit of the other residents, I think it quite advisable. You are not a common street person, Paula. Why set yourself up as such?"

"You sound just like that damned policeman."

"Why not? He is as aware of the opinions of others as anyone I know. Do YOU think your actions are above reproach? Is being a prostitute your ultimate goal?"

What are you? Some kind of a preacher?"

"No, Paula, I am just a man watching a lovely girl taking a nose-dive into oblivion by her heedlessness and lack of control of her emotions. I see a friend directing her life into a no-win course that has but one ending. What do you see?"

"Oh, GET LOST!"

"No. I don't plan to take that detour, Paula. As a matter of fact, I hope I am not too late to turn my life around and find a hereafter with a happier outcome. What do you hope for, Paula?" Her control evaporated, and she fled to her apartment in tears. Pete's distress was evident in his slumped shoulders and his slow progress to his front door.

Before entering, he stopped. Things were moving far too fast for his mind to assimilate. There was just too much, too fast, and in too many directions. For once, his normal reasoning seemed unattainable. Where was he supposed to begin to untangle things? For that matter, what, exactly, were the tangles of priority position?

Jelly beans? Police visits? Unreliable lease forms? Laundry room security? Mrs. Strickland and her bothersome tale? What? His problems were unlike any ball of thread or coil of rope which might be followed from point A to point B and on to an end. These unrelated and noxious obstacles arrived alone and resisted any effort which might solve them.His eyes wandered from apartment number twenty, to the pool and up again.

Chapter VI

Love comes back to his vacant dwelling,
The old, old love that we knew of yore!
Henry Austin Dobson

His glance toward the upper level revealed Paula's door being held open by Patti. whose words clearly were meant to be heard.

"Don't let our pious landlord frighten you, Paula. He has no legal right to interfere with you or your activities. Your date was terribly sorry he frightened you. What did they do to you at the station?"

The memory of being interrogated prompted Paula's tears to overrun their boundaries once more.

"Oh Patti, it was awful!" Tears that had been waiting their turn began to roll.

"Did they quiz you about Pris and me and the guys next door? Patti pressed for information.

"Yes, and they wanted to know how well we knew Mr. LaBanta. They acted like they know he furnishes the stuff we give to our dates."

"You didn't tell them, did you?" Patti's voice was lowered until Paula could but faintly hear her.

"I don't think I told them anything, but they kept asking me over and over in different words and even letting one after another take turns in questioning me." Paula's tears reached flood stage once more.

Patti was unsure how she might help, but she tried.

"I have a sandwich if you want it. I know you must be hungry, aren't you?"

"Not really. Besides, I saw Kelly in the pool. Maybe she could give me some swimming pointers. Do you want to come along?"

"I don't think so, but you go ahead. I have a date in a little while. Patti was doing her best to discern the direction of Paula's thoughts. "Are you available for guests?"

"NO! All I want is to go swimming." Paula ran into the bathroom and slammed the door.

In less than five minutes, she was back and on her way down the stairs. Patti gave up and walked away from the window.

Kelly Richardson had had a long day at the club, and it showed. Even though her swim suit was the same vibrant one she wore for the pool party, she moved like she had aged many years since that gala affair. She entered the pool from the corner steps.

Seeing her there, Pete wondered if he would be a welcome guest at her private party.His mind had just about given its permission when he saw Paula approaching the pool. Perhaps not just now, he thought to himself. How in the world was he ever going to handle the numerous problems that seemed to be recreating themselves at every attempt to alleviate them. As Paula stepped into the water, Pete stepped into his apartment. The defeated shrug to his shoulders made its own announcement.

In Number twenty across the way, Mrs. Strickland stood at her window and watched the activity below. Her lips compressed into a thin, determined line.

"That girl needs help," she said to the draperies as she headed for the door. By the time she reached the stone bench near the pool, Kelly was welcoming Paula's company, and Pete, drawing back from his window, uttered "RATS!"

His stride to his desk was wrapped in frustration. Reaching for mail needing his attention, his eyes became riveted to the movement of the paper. Then the paper exploded and a little, gray mouse leaped down and became invisible behind the filing cabinet. Pete Newman inhaled a deep breath to dislodge the fright he had come through.

"WOW!" That was one thing he could not tolerate, MICE. He reached for the business section of the telephone book to look for a name of an exterminator He must alert Frank to keep an eye out for other signs of infestation..

In the meantime, Mrs. Strickland was thinking of her upcoming talk. with Pete. At some time she intended to tell Pete Newman about his father's background; that seeming to be his major question of life. Right now was not the time. She would know when to open the subject. She was sincere about her concern for Paula even if Pete didn't see things as she did. She looked out at the pool again and watched Kelly giving the girl some pointers on swimming.

"Beautiful!" she called, clapping for their performance. Kelly is making a friend of the girl, and that is commendable. Her thoughts included plans to assist the process.

"Kelly is a good woman even if Pete cannot see it. She could be exactly what he needs to be a happy man. Yes, and Paula could be outstanding in any field if only she had a chance and the desire". Ida Mae Strickland sighed. She approved the pattern of her thoughts and left the rest of the world to continue to on its destructive course. She felt utterly lost in her ability to twist life into the shape she was positive it needed to be. She waved to the swimmers.

"You two make a beautiful scene. Keep it up, and you will be ready for the Olympics."

Back in her apartment, she took her yellow writing pad to the table and sat, pen in hand, to jot notes she would later organize to tell the whole story in an understandable fashion. She liked the words her pen deposited before her.

"I was sixteen years old, and he was eighteen, the very cream of what our government sought when war became inevitable," she wrote. In a way, he was the epitome of American pride, like all young recruits. I was in love. We had known each other all of our lives, and he had all of the ideal qualifications to promise a forever after existence. Memories washed over the older lady. Through misty eyes she could recall his touch and almost hear the tenderness of his voice. She laid the pen across the unfinished page and stood. As though it would all return if she could just keep the memory alive, she walked to the kitchen and heated a cup of the morning's left-over coffee. It might organize her thinking.

She sat at the little kitchen table and relived the last time she had shared a picnic lunch with him. Springtime! The first tulips blooming in the park! The fresh scent of newly mowed grass filling the air around them. And, then his kiss!

"He held my hands in both of his and, his eyes commanded mine to meet his. He told me he loved me.

"I love you, Ida Mae, and I want us to be married." He dropped my right hand and reached into his pocket to produce a simple, gold ring. He slid it onto my left hand. I knew then that my future would always be melded to his.

"Do you feel the same as I do?"

The memory stirred her emotions. With her heart responding as it had when she was sixteen, Ida Mae brushed at her moist eyes and gazed across the years. So clearly could she feel his nearness that she answered as she had then.

"Yes. Yes, of course I do." The words came bursting from my lips. I could not have had another answer. There was no other answer. There was nothing but our love.

With his arms still holding me close, he added:

"Ida Mae, tomorrow at sunup my service duty begins. My name is on the list of those to be shipped early. We have only tonight we can call our own."

I was stunned. Even his promises to return could not calm the fears which marched like angry rulers through my mind. Nor could his next kiss recreate my joy. Only his love could seal the promises we made that evening. We would always belong to each other.

Ida took the coffee cup to the sink and herded her struggling thoughts back to the yellow pad. She sat for several minutes before lifting the pen to continue.

"Shortly after he left, I discovered I was pregnant. I managed to finish school by wearing loose fitting clothes. Morning sickness was 'the flu', and I seemed to have a lot of it during those early months. I wrote to your dad to tell him we were going to be parents. I knew he would be happy to receive that news, but he did not answer that letter, nor the next, nor the next several. I finally concluded that he no longer cared for me. I was devastated. I felt used and abandoned. I wanted no part of his child. Never did it cross my mind that I could have an abortion. This was my own flesh and blood. I insisted that I wanted to let it be adopted by someone who wouldn't have these memories to overcome.

My family was heart broken, but they stood by me. They offered to take the baby. It was, after all, their grandchild, but I would not allow that. Instead, I agreed to complete my nine months in an adoption home that would see me through my difficult days and would then find a family to take the baby.

Something foreign seemed to be born in my personality. I wanted only to be left alone, free to become frigid and hard.

"I heard the baby's first cries as it was torn from my body, and I asked to see him just once.Even though I had signed away that right, I just could not give him away. I kept screaming, 'Please, PLEASE' until the nurse reminded me that I was an unwed mother and had already admitted I could not handle the responsibility. I continued to scream until the whole staff was trying to reason with me.The doctor suggested that I let the baby be brought up in a foster home instead of being adopted. I did not realize at that time that I had only to give the name of the child's father, and the adoption would have been stopped.

"By then, I would have agreed to anything except adoption. They warned me I would not be allowed to have any contact with the child. I could not feed him or dress or hold him, and I could never let him know I was his mother. They would keep him until he was three years old before letting him be adopted. If my circumstances changed in that time and I wanted to take him, that might be arranged. My family helped me to make that decision. In the meantime, I was provided with a room in exchange for doing house or office work, or whatever they needed that I could do."I didn't think they could legally hold me to that promise, but I agreed. I was able to watch his development. I did not break my promise by cuddling, or touching. I was grateful to be able to watch him grow, to have a paying job and to be near him. The arrangement was against all policies of the foundation, and I was grateful for that leniency. I am sure my parents had a hand in my good fortune.

I was not aware that your father also was walking a difficult path at that time. Following the ordeal of being shot during the first week of his experience abroad, he was left with a mind which, for a time, vacillated between consciousness and sleep. He was treated by a caring nurse who helped him to accept the fact that his leg was gone. His loss of memory at that time protected him from feeling the same loss that I was feeling. His gentle manners helped him to recover his physical health in time, and his gratitude toward the caring lady who had nursed him through the ordeal became his main concern. Temporary memory loss held him in rigid chains. He neither remembered me nor knew that I existed. If he had a feeling of incompleteness, he attributed it to having lost a leg. He married his benefactor without ever knowing that I had given birth to his son.

" My own feeling was more bafflement than hate. The blame I felt was embarrassment at having been so gullible; yet, at the same time, I could not totally convince myself of his infidelity. I lived our last time together over and over and over. Nothing changed the facts.

"I had no idea that he was struggling just to live after losing his leg. I had no way of knowing that the kindness of that special nurse was keeping him alive.

When he was considered healed enough to return to the United States, he was discharged and given two tickets and a lump sum settlement for his loss. With this he made a substantial payment on this apartment complex. It was newly finished just weeks before his return. It provided a home for both of them, as well as an income for some time. It was when his wife's health began to fail that the duties became insurmountable, a regular part of their days after she became pregnant and learned that her body was not strong enough to have a normal birth. Things became so difficult, in fact, that she could not continue to help him run the business. She could no longer clean the apartments; cooking turned her into a nauseous heap, and rising before mid-day was an ordeal too demanding for her frailty.The garden grass began to die for lack of attention, and his spirits sagged under the unaccustomed demands of management. Still they made every attempt to survive.

When their little girl was born, the tasks grew, and the woman's health deteriorated more rapidly. Her parents took the baby to their home in Ohio until her strength could return. She did not mend. Instead, her feeble condition worsened, demanding greater care in their unavailable time.

"I think it was sheer desperation that caused your dad to place a newspaper ad for an assistant manager. When the office staff at the foster home read that ad, they suggested that I apply for the position. His name was not mentioned; so I could not be forewarned of Fate's plans.The staff was so hopeful and so helpful, even to seeing that I was appropriately dressed for the interview, that I began to think this might be the opening I sought." Little did I guess then how much our former pledges would continue to surround us until we had fulfilled the promises made. That lesson was learned in the forthcoming months and years ahead.

This remembrance pushed the lady's hand away from the yellow pad once more. She sat far back in her chair and took a deep breath to fuel her lengthy sigh. Then she wrote, "You cannot possibly imagine the shock which enveloped both of us when I walked into his office. I wanted to run. I wanted to stay. I could only stare at this man who had been the very core of my universe so long ago. I started toward the door, but he objected.

"Let's at least catch up. Shall we?'

"I had no choice but to agree.

To partly eliminate the awkwardness facing us, he pulled up his pants leg and displayed his prosthesis as he added: 'A one-legged man can't do you much damage, now, can he? Sit down and tell me your story. You already know parts of mine.' He laughed. 'At lease the artificial part of it.'

"What could I do but laugh with him?"Still the same wit and the same courage I had seen in him in our youth. So I sat, and we visited for a bit before he broached the real issue of this meeting."

"My wife is a lovely lady, Ida Mae. I am convinced it was her concern and care that kept me alive during a time when I had no way of knowing how gravely ill I was. She has seen me through indescribable odds, and she agreed to marry me and to help me back into the business of living. Now it is my time to do the same for her. Her body was simply too frail to nurture our baby, a fair haired little girl, and, unless I can find the right help for her, my wife won't make it, either. I need to be with her, or have someone to be with her. I cannot do an adequate job of running this place nor of helping her. As things stand at this time, I cannot do ANYTHING! Can you think of any way you can help? Become our manager and maybe now and then help with her a little? Ida Mae, I'm a desperate man. Please?"

Even as these glimpses into her past tumbled through her heart, Mrs. Strickland continued to write as though she were telling the story aloud.

"All I could think about was that I was there facing a man who had lost his child and who could conceivably lose his wife, as well. Yes, I felt a yearning for the past that could not be regained, but I had lost a child, too. I just couldn't do what he was asking, but neither could I refuse to help him.

"If you could see your way clear to help, I think you would like my wife, Ida Mae. She is so ill, and she needs constant care. Would you consider a furnished apartment with all bills paid, plus a salary to take over both duties? I know that's asking a lot of you, but...would you?"

"That's how I wound up being Assistant Manager for your dad. And getting to know your mom was truly one of the richest experiences in my life. She rallied for a time. and began to talk about having another baby. She knew she could probably never have another, and that knowledge haunted her day and night.

"Finally, I suggested that your dad adopt an older child so she could transfer her grief onto someone other than herself. I even suggested that he call the foster home that I knew would likely have one that he would love. Your dad liked the idea. He even felt that a son might be good for both of them. He was so enthusiastic about the idea that I said I would take more responsibility for the running of the apartments so that he could assist in bonding with the child. Fortunately, his wife eagerly agreed, and he asked me to check on the matter.

"You can imagine how quickly I took care of that detail! Within a minimum of time, you had been given your present name. What a joyful home it became. Your mother improved enough for them to move into a house with a yard, and you became her main reason for facing each new day.

"I functioned as Apartment Manager. I also became 'that cranky old lady' who lived upstairs." Mrs. Strickland laid the pen down again and looked into a distant past. She pushed the yellow pad to the back of the table and walked back to the window to gaze outside as though she might forget the pain of watching another woman accept the reins of parenthood while she, herself, was left with no place to bestow her own affections.

I think I served as a good lookout for them," she said aloud. "And I felt a sense of great loss when she died." She thought of getting another cup of coffee, but remembering the last cup, she made a disapproving face. It was cold. So was her eagerness to write more of this painful story at this time. But it needed to be written, she admitted. It would be a greater burden than she had the strength to endure if she was forced to orally relate this story to Pete. She would write it, and she would wait until the appropriate time to give it to Peter Newman, her son.

Rubbing her hands across eyes that were puffy with weariness, she leaned her elbows on the desk top before picking up the pen. She MUST finish this one chore, and soon.

"You were enrolled in a boarding school. The house was closed, and your dad moved back into the apartment downstairs. We worked well together. There was never a thought of romance on his part or mine. The events in our lives had given to both of us an understanding and tolerance we might never have had without them. We were old friends, and a solid friendship is far more valuable than a warmed over love affair.

"You came home on regular breaks at school. You know the rest." She paused. Then she continued with determination to let the story slide it's way past the unbearable scene of the death of her son's father, so soon, so very soon after his wife's demise.

"I made a feeble attempt to relieve the pain I saw in your eyes, but you shunned my interest. After your father's death, I accepted the fact that I would always be 'that bossy old woman' to you. I was convinced you would be needing my guidance. How very little I realized how urgently I needed to stay close to you! Little by little the relationship between us stabilized and merged into its current pattern. We were destined to be together for the rest of our lives, and I believe that destiny was established the night you were conceived.

Mrs. Strickland tucked the yellow pad into a desk drawer. She had written as much as her emotions would allow for today. She walked to the window and looked out. Pete was talking to Frank Fisher in the garden below. 'Pete looks awfully tired,' she thought.

"He is being pulled into too many directions lately! It would be so good if he could just relax and take Kelly to dinner, or even give in to an evening of television with her." Another of her long sighs escaped tightly drawn lips.

Her window of opportunity had long been closed, nor would it again open to her.

Like Moses, she had reached her promised land only to learn she was unable to dwell in it.

Mrs. Strickland drew the curtains and turned her back on the outside world. The outside world continued its forward direction as Pete and Frank chatted.

Each man noticed the uniformed locksmith enter the courtyard. Pete strode over to meet him as the service man spoke.

"I believe I'm the man you are looking for. Right?"

"Yes. I am Pete Newman, the one who called you. Would you like to see the laundry room first?

"First AND last, if I understood your needs correctly. You want a new lock, and you want new keys for every apartment? Is that right?"

"Unless you have another suggestion that will serve the purpose of preventing unauthorized persons using the machines."

"There are two other ways to do that. One is to make one key which you keep in the office to lend out when a tenant wants to use it. Another is to make the tenants' keys fit the laundry room door and also their individual units. This way is a bit more expensive, I admit, but it would cover your need. It would also require changing the locks on all apartments"

"I think a new lock and enough keys for my sixty units ought to suffice." Pete could imagine this job lasting and lasting and lasting.

"But that will mean you have to keep up with that many more issued keys. You don't want to have to be retagging every single key, do you? Better go along with the idea of one key per unit, don't you think?" The Smithy argued.

"NO, I DON'T THINK. Can you get started making the individual keys right away?" The nerves running up Pete's neck tightened. Did this guy actually think he could dictate the terms of this deal? He regretted his hasty answer at once.

"I'm sorry," he apologized. There have been so many trains jumping the tracks around here recently that I am getting a bit testy."

"No problem, sir. I'll get on with your order at once."

Pete's head began its habitual shake as the locksmith put his attention to the task at hand. He rubbed the back of his neck, wondering why the past several months seemed to bring out his least likable personality traits.

"I probably ought to take a vacation, but where would I go and what would I do?

I don't fish. I don't hunt nor enjoy camping. I wouldn't know which end of a golf club to use to hit the ball. A tour, maybe? Why? Sight a seeing tour could be a big bore with no one to share it with." He thought of Kelly Richardson.

"I wonder what a Mediterranean tour would be like with her along," He was still smiling at such an improbable supposition by the time he reached his unit, but he knew he would never have an opportunity to enter a dream like that. Still, entertaining the thought of getting away for a short time had a certain magnetic appeal.

Mrs. Strickland would take care of things if he did decide to take a few days off.

She knew the business, maybe better than he did, but if anyone deserved time to get away, it would certainly be her, not himself. Even so, what would a vacation have to do with his disposition going south? Pete Newman was anything but pleased with most recent snappishness. First things, FIRST! On his way to the office, he saw Gene Seals coming through the back entry; and, at Gene's gesture, he waited for the mechanic to approach.

"Pete, I was hoping to see you. I have a fourteen year old grand daughter who is bugging me to ask your permission to swim in the pool. Any objections?"

"Not as long as you are with her. My insurance man wouldn't take too kindly to being held responsible for a teenager drowning. I hope you understand."

"I certainly do. I've noticed Paula likes to swim, and I thought it might be good if my girl could take a few pointers from her or even from Kelly, for that matter. But the girl needs to have another girl she can relate to, and the more I see of Paula taking charge of her own life, the more I think her influence could be good for this tadpole of mine."

Pete frowned for a moment.

"Well, let's play it by the rules, Gene. Paula cannot be considered as an adult to be held responsible. As long as you are doing life guard duty, it's OK."

"Thanks, Pete. We appreciate your situation. We'll hold the line on it. By the way, her name is Fran Seals. I may have to scrape her off the ceiling when she hears about this."

Pete turned toward his previous destination, intent on opening the conversation with Mrs. Strickland, until Gene claimed his attention again.

Chapter VII

Great God, I ask thee for no meaner pelf,
Than in my action, I may soar as high as I can discern
With this clear eye.
Washington Irving

"What I really came over to tell you is that the part we've been looking for is in.

If you can spare your car for about an hour, I'll run it over and take care of that right now."

The laundry room door was standing open. Pete entered and was instantly accosted by the acrid odor of smoke and water damaged walls. They would have to be replaced. What about the machines? They were owned by a laundry equipment business in exchange for the money paid into the coin boxes with each use. Would the owners replace the machines? If not, would they clean them? One thing was certain. He DID NOT WANT TO OWN THE MACHINES. He wouldn't know how to repair them they needed it, and he didn't have time to go to some class to learn how. Let the company take care of that problem. Remembering that he had not notified the equipment owners of the fire, he snapped his fingers to jolt his memory into action. He should do that right now. And NEXT he would get a painter scheduled to start painting A.S.A.P. Perhaps he should use one of the service members of the apartment association.

His feet chose the direction of his next move. Though he was not conscious of a plan to see Mrs. Strickland just yet, he found himself on the upper landing leading to number twenty. Had he intended to see her? For what? There was a strange memory or something that kept eluding him. He almost believed he was remembering a past part of his life. It was like the first meeting of Chary and himself and each finding a mutual familiarity in the encounter. Sometimes he wondered if he really knew this guy named Peter Newman.

Strangely, he usually sought the company of Mrs. Strickland when events overlapped. It seemed so natural to listen to her point of view even though there was that ever present urge to disagree with her. WHY?

Whenever there was a need for action, she was there. Just now, for instance, her concern was genuine as she called down to offer assistance if needed. Face it. "I must be the biggest heel in the universe to shove her offers back in her face." Pete was being visited by an over active conscience. What a fool he was!

He shook his head to clear the confusion, and descended the steps one at a time, slowly, carefully, coming down to the level where he lived. His head was shaking from one side to the other at the thought of this incredulous person, Mrs. Strickland. How mistaken he had been! Mistaken, ashamed and regretful for years of friendship lost in his ignorance. His distress was evident in his frown and his slow progress toward his apartment. He ran his hands through his hair again as if the effort might eliminate the past.

August burned it's way into September, that special month that followed its own agenda of being hot and being cold, of promising the coming of Fall while ending the unfulfilled promises of summer. Pete had always looked forward to the 'smell of September' which was prevalent for only one day each year, the time for the Purple Martins to gather on the telephone lines over the city and chatter about their southern travel. Vacations came to an end in that magical month. Brain power, born to the marriage of restful vacation and renewed plans for the future, surged with determination and desire.

October was Nature's way of cleaning house; Mrs. Strickland had told him that when he was just a small boy.

"She puts away her pretty pinks and soft yellow dresses and wears colors that will warm her bones when cold, damp days arrive." Pete never forgot that story. The lady did not have a matching story for November; it was its own saga needing nothing to advertise it. Because there were no children, if one didn't count the expected babe, Halloween wandered away unrecognized by the denizens of the apartment complex. Porch lights were conspicuous by their absent emanation. There would be no 'Tricks or Treats tonight. November poked its head through the pages of the calendars, and all thoughts turned toward Thanksgiving. Some knew why. Others did not. Birthday celebrations left footprints in the sands and waves of time. Heavier coats and occasional boots became the uniform of the day. Pilgrims and pumpkins appeared in windows and entryways. Smoke from individual grills embroidered the skies and drew smiles from witnesses. Thanksgiving sales drew crowds and dollars to inflate the local economy.

Pete welcomed the heating and plumbing persons who would make sure all systems were producing properly. Recalling his skirmish with Mrs. Strickland when her air conditioning was not working, he shook his head and grinned. She had been so right, and he had been so wrong. Even his familiar shaking of his head offered no relief from the guilt which overcame him at such times.

Christmas advertisements vied for attention on the pages of the local papers. Life in the apartments was little changed from what it had earlier been; yet there was a subtle difference this year. The residents were less eager to enter the race for the most money spent, or the greatest number of lights exhibited. The general atmosphere was one of a more hopeful and serious thought than had been noticed in the past. A change had come to the residents of the Apartments. There was more sincerity in the greetings as they passed one another, and the good will expressed in those greetings was mutual. Truly the Spirit of Christmas was descending upon this group. Christmas cards were daily mailbox stuffers. The nippy November air quickened the steps of the heart-happy tenants even as their calendars filled with more activities.

Noticeable was the difference in the activities in the three second floor apartments these days. Fewer male visitors were in evidence in the evenings when the Peas were at home. The wintry chill discouraged much outside movement, and as though they had been cautioned to be less vocal, the two men in adjoining apartments were seldom seen. The noise of their frequent parties in the past months was soon forgotten.

Quite often, Pete could be seen knocking on door of number twenty That lady renewed her long ago practice of attending early church services on Sundays, and Pete volunteered to be her chauffeur whenever needed. On a few special days he attended services with her. At an earlier time, He had belittled the lady's constant genealogy research. Somehow, now, her need to confirm her heredity seemed right. It fit the new picture . There was always a chart showing new erasures and additions. Her collection of books relating to the areas involved were at hand but she had not shared the contents of her chart.

Remembering their promise to have their little talk later, Pete asked her one cold November day, "Are we ready to finish that conversation that was interrupted by the fire?""It will keep," she answered and changed the subject. Pete assumed 'it would keep' But he wondered about her past life, as well as his own, for that matter.

'What might life have been like if she had been his mother', he wondered when he visited her. How different would his memories be? How differently might his personality have been molded? Peter Newman was far too reticent to mention those thoughts, but they persisted in being his inquisitor.

There was something else he COULD do, though, while there were yet a few balmy Fall days. The idea came as his eyes roamed over the colorful pansies that Frank Fisher had planted Too soon the area would wear its drab and leafless winter coat.

"Mrs. Strickland, let's have a barbecue. You can already smell winter on its way. What do you say to that?"

"Why, I think that is a wonderful idea, Peter. When do you have in mind?"

"Right this very Sunday afternoon Are you in favor of that?"

"Oh, my. We'd better get Miss Richardson to help don't you think?"

That is fine if you will do the asking. I always say the wrong things to her."

"Well, try asking the right questions and see what happens." She did not attempt to disguise the humorous intent in her words. She had called him Peter. Pete wondered if Mrs. Strickland realized she had not said "Mr. Newman."

As expected, the barbecue agenda was well on its way by the time the last tenant had been called.

There was another door that opened to Pete's knocks these days. Paula did not have the male visitors she once had, and Pete saw to it that she was made a welcome guest at any of the Apartment weekend galas. He was pleased that Paula had welcomed the idea of helping the young Seals girl with her swimming.

She was keeping some distance between herself and her former friends. If she was not visiting with Mrs. Strickland, she often might be seen in the garden area, sometimes quietly walking and at other times talking with Frank Fisher. Mrs. Strickland made it a point to join Paula whenever the occasion allowed, and so the healing power of withdrawal worked its wonders. If she was concerned about paying her next month's rent, none could detect it.

"Oh, what fun!" Paula responded to Pete's suggestion, then her face lost its joyful look. "But I am a little bit broke right now. Maybe some other time?"

" Don't worry about buying something, Paula. But you WILL help us get it going, won't you?"

"Certainly, Pete. I'll be glad to help, but I don't want to butt in when I can't pay my way." The sincerity of her words curled up inside Pete's heart. His outstretched hand ended with a friendly pat on her shoulder.

"I notice you were helping young Fran Seals with her swimming on a few warm days we have had. Would you like to ask her to be your guest at the barbecue?"

"You don't think I might lead her the wrong way?" There was a painful irony in the question.

"Paula, if every person who ever made a mistake was held down by it, even after she was displaying serious intention to reform, the world would be in a terrible shape. Your sincerity is noticed by all of us. We don't think of your mistakes every time we look at you, and you should not think such things when we include you in activities. If you ask Fran Seals to join us, we will all welcome her AS YOUR FRIEND. If you choose to not ask her, no one is going to put a tag on your intention. It is possible that girl needs a friend near her own age, and you might find that doing something for someone else could aid your own endeavors."

"I'm sorry, Pete. Thank you. I will ask her. Paula was smiling as she watched her landlord continuing on his earlier mission.

The timing was right. Mutual enjoyment spread like a common cold. The attendance was complete, and the long, folding tables, hauled up from the basement recreation room, threatened to sag with the abundance of food. The sweet smell of barbecuing brisket intensified the frolicsome atmosphere.

"WOW! Does that make you salivate, or WHAT?" Frank inhaled deeply as he tested the meat with a probe. "It will be ready by the time everyone gets a bib tied around his neck"

Gene Seals appeared at the back entrance with long handled fork and tongs as well as an additional bag of briquettes.

"Think you can use these?" He held the tools up for approval.

"JUST WHAT WE NEED, GENE, AND RIGHT ON TIME!" Frank took the offering and made a show of giving them prime space on the barbecue rack. "WHO'S GOT THE COW BELL?"

From one of the lower apartments came the clang of the bell which,long ago, had been designated as 'THE COW BELL' and used to summon all bulls and cows. None ever knew when the bell first gained such prominence; nor did any, except the thief, notice who picked it up to be used at another get together on yet another day. It always appeared when someone asked about it, and it disappeared before the final goodnight.

Charles Reasoner was the one aloof member of this mellow group. He continued to display his fears of authority and overt friendliness. Pete's attempts at convincing his neighbor to repay friendly overtures in like kind resulted in more withdrawal. He joined his neighbors for the barbecue around the pool for a while. Suddenly, he simply was not there. It would be some time before Charley Reasoner reappeared. During that time, the pace of life at the apartment complex seemed to move more rapidly.

"Football, anyone?" Another Thanksgiving Day was properly ended. As the football fans headed for the office to watch the game on television, Fran Seals joined Paula in the final cleaning of utensils and of food storage.

Gene Seals put in an appearance just in time to move the tables back to the basement storage room. As they closed the door and retraced their steps to the garden area, he produced a box of chocolates as their reward. His glance at Frank contained the question of the fitness of the gift. Frank's nod was one of assurance.

The surprised acceptance on Paula's face finished the unspoken question. One more Thanksgiving day ended with grateful hearts, filled stomachs, and hints of future pleasure.Then came the snows. None could remember when there had been snow banks reaching the ledges of the first floor windows or snow falling so silently and in such abundance. Traffic was halted. Schools were closed. Newspapers and other deliveries were late or non-existent. Youths with sleds that had remained unseen prior to this enforced vacation were now as numerous as overcoats and head wraps. Despite the many lists so meticulously made for Christmas shopping, most downtown stores were closed, and those remaining open were empty of customers. Across the soundless city could be heard the bells of the local churches summoning worshipers to accept this extraordinary opportunity.

Surprisingly, it was Charles Reasoner who mobilized the action.

"Hey, let's all go to church," he proposed.

The unexpected invitation was welcomed by most of the residents, and within minutes, while winding a path down the middle of the road, they were singing with the tunes provided by the bell tower some blocks away. That glorious spirit of the Christ child's birth was working its ages-old magic in the hearts of all. Paula joined the festive walk, keeping close to Mrs. Strickland, a bit away from Pete. Most of the residents who did not join this unfettered party came out and waved the singers on their way. Chary was prominently in the lead. Especially noticeable was the cheerful attempt of the group's oldest member, Mrs. Strickland, refusing help. She was childlike in her delight. Nor did her raspy voice miss a word of the familiar songs they sang.

"Oh, I've never enjoyed anything more than this," she laughed.

"Don't get too tired, though. We want you to be able to enjoy many more fun days like this." Kelly's admonition was ignored, and Mrs. Strickland sang even more lustily than before.

The younger ones indulged their gaming instincts with snowballs, and lively phonation pierced the walls of buildings as they passed. Laughing approval from on-lookers encouraged the parading songsters.

As though awaiting this very congregation, the doors of the church in the next block were thrown open, and the cleric waved the throng inside. Pete and Paula each reached for an arm to assist Mrs. Strickland up the three steps to the door.

"My, I DO feel protected", her frosty words were delivered through visible breath.Stomping snow from their shoes, they entered. The scent of fresh pine boughs on the sills of the stained glass windows sharpened their expectant feelings. If the worshipers were a bit early this year, they were none the less welcomed by the Spirit that was timely indeed. Laughter and playfulness fell from the visiting seekers, and a reverent respect took over. The hush was akin to the silent snows. The warmth of the chapel heat matched the feeling of love and comradeship which permeated the visitors.

Without introduction, the Pastor opened his message by saying:

"I have always known that when the students are ready, the teacher appears. I see that you are ready, and you see that I have appeared. Please open the hymnal to page 333, and let us sing a verse of 'Joy To the World.'

Never was that song more lustily sung, and, for the next twenty minutes, the group again heard the ages-old story. The robed speaker looked at the assemblage before adding to the message.

"Each of you came here this afternoon in search of something. I trust the message has given peace."

Then it was over. A more thoughtful assemblage filed out of the church and began their walk toward home. The sound of silence covered their world. Only their individual thoughts communicated.

"Oh Holy night...oh night divine...."

Pete took Mrs. Strickland's arm to assist her down the road, but it was Paula for whose arm she reached as she forced one foot after another. 'Think on these things", he thought to himself as he stepped aside. Kelly fell into step with Pete as he relinquished his place to Paula.

"Will I do as a replacement?" She tucked her arm through his. A slight quiver wound its way down his spine. Why did she have to be so desirable?

"Will I do as a replacement for your handsome Mr. LaBanta?" He really hadn't meant for his voice to sound as cold as it did. He felt like a fool, an oaf, an idiot!

"Only if you can afford the salary he pays me," she teased.

"This is not a laughing matter, Kelly. You don't see him for what he is."

"And WHAT might that be?"

"He's a thug, Kelly, and you are smart enough to see it."

Kelly's arm dropped away from his. She stepped a pace away and turned toward him."Maybe I don't have your brand of intelligence, Peter Newman, and maybe that is a good thing. You can think anything you want to think, but don't expect me or anyone else to echo your dislike. I think you missed the whole message we all heard minutes ago." With that she turned and matched her stride to that of Frank Fisher. Pete rammed his fists into his pants pockets...deeply into those pockets. Would he ever in this whole world learn to control his tongue? He had practically called her a liar. He hated himself!

It was Paula who assisted Mrs. Strickland up the stairs and opened the door for her friend. She helped her inside and into a chair in the warmth of her familiar surroundings. It was Paula who offered to make tea, and it was the grateful older lady who admitted that she was as tired as she appeared to be.

The warm spirit of the group's earlier response to the parson's words seemed now to be forgotten. Even Chary grew non-communicative with his landlord in the next days.

The snow remained and was refreshed by new layers nightly. Two weeks before Christmas, Nature promised to continue the awesomeness of the season. More snow fell. Drifts appeared higher and higher on the trees and buildings and even the telephone wires. Christmas trees were alight in most of the apartment windows. Christmas music escaped the units when doors were opened. A huge snowman appeared in the courtyard, and Frank swept walkways and stair steps again and again and again. Truly, a winter wonderland emerged where a mundane world existed.

Pete was uncommonly quiet as he attended his routine duties. He was aware of carols being sung in various apartments. Everyone wanted Chary to join them, and his response was instant. Later in the evenings, the camaraderie continued in various apartments as though all shared some special thoughts which belonged only to the season... thoughts which had so stirred his own heart. Pete was caught in a trap of his own making. He regretted his outburst to Kelly, and he could think of no way to undo the damage it had caused. He welcomed the quiet of his abode only to find that the very silence pointed an accusing finger at him. Tomorrow would be soon enough to visit. The next few days continued to be filled with these somber thoughts. Food did not appeal to him. Sleep abandoned him, and his conscience was choking him. Peter Newman had played the role of a fool.

The temperature dropped into the low thirties that night, and little activity could be seen in the courtyard. Pete would have made coffee had there been any coffee. There was none. Neither coffee nor bread nor anything else that he considered edible. It was too early to disturb the tenants, and he needed a cup of coffee. He chose to not awaken Mrs. Strickland to ask what she needed from the grocery store. He pulled on his heaviest jacket and left. He would pick up a few things she might want.

Driving required total concentration to avoid a mishap in the fresh fallen snow that had swallowed the road edges and curbs. He would stock up on everything while he was out. The only parking place he found was at least a block away from the door.

Once inside the store, he scanned every shelf on every aisle. Many of the items in his cart were for Mrs. Strickland. He would make sure she had some of the extras for the holiday season. For himself he loaded up on frozen dinners, fruit, cereal and coffee...plenty of coffee.

"You can always spot a married man", teased the cashier. "Your wife gave you quite a list today, didn't she?"

Married? Himself? He had not thought about a basket of groceries being identified with marriage. He grinned.

"She certainly did, didn't she?"

He was still grinning to himself as he loaded the groceries in the trunk of his car.

Wondering what it would be like to be married, he grew more sober. No, he couldn't even imagine being a married man, living with a woman. Not even living with somebody like Kelly. Better dismiss that idea, he decided. He pulled in to his parking space and pushed the button to open the trunk. He shivered as the blast of cold air slapped his face.

His grin faded at the thought of his stupid behavior.

"Rats!" He began to unload the groceries. It would take several trips to move all of them. Why had he not separated the ones for Mrs. Strickland as he loaded them? Pete stacked several sacks together and started toward the gate. Turning to see whether he had closed the car door, the oranges shifted weight. One after the other they rolled under the car far enough away that he must kneel to retrieve them.

The can of coffee followed.

Pulling himself upright again, the distraught man took the first of many steps to his ground floor unit. To open his door, it was necessary to use the key he had already deposited in his pants pocket. Rigid hands set the parcels on the walkway by his door as he performed this activity.

The wind continued to blow. Pete's ill humor continued to rise. The paper bags continued to disintigrate. A determined man began the sodden chore of reclaiming every item and wrestling them to his door. Peter Newman was not going to allow mere grocery items to dictate his attitude. This decision appeared to have the desired result. At last all purchases were lodged in his kitchen, some on the cabinets and some on the floor.

Chapter VIII

Leaves have their time to fall, and flowers to wither at the Northwind's breath, and stars to set- but all, thou hasty all seasons for thine own. O death!
Felicia Hemans

Yes It was easier to take all of the groceries into his kitchen than to climb the stairs. He would take things to Mrs. Strickland later. Right now he would make a pot of coffee!

He hoped she would approve of his selection for her; there was more than he had realized he was buying, especially so many ready-to-eat items. Well, she could share them with some of the tenants like Kelly and Paula. Right now he was reacting to the scent of fresh brewed coffee.

He poured a cup, opened a package of sweet rolls and pulled his chair out in readiness for a feast. The telephone! Chary could stand a cup of coffee if Pete happened to have any. Pete did. He shook his head and grinned. It was great to have his neighbor back in his teasing form.

Three hours later, when Pete's telephone was silent for most of the day, he called Mrs. Strickland. He frowned. It was not like her to be out in this weather. He dialed again. Still there was no answer; so he donned his jacket once more. When the door was not opened at his knock, he used his master key. In the big lounge chair, half-sitting, half-lying, the older lady lay clutching a bottle of vapor salve and unsuccessfully attempting to raise her hand and to speak. Her genealogy chart lay on the table, awaiting her next addition.

Pete ran to touch and reassure her as he retrieved the blanket, which had fallen from her shoulders. Noticing the writing pad with Paula's name and number, he dialed for her help. His hand on the lady's forehead told him the fever was too high to be a mere cold. The sound of Paula's running steps preceded her hasty entrance. While she soothed her friend with words and soft touch, Pete dialed 911. Within five minutes the patient was loaded, and Paula was with her, all action progressing like scenes in a play, logical and timely but leaving the audience with a sense of unreality.

Pete went through the apartment, securing doors and turning off lights. Noticing the absence of breakfast dishes, tears ran unchecked down his cheeks. WHY IN THE WORLD HAD HE WAITED SO LONG BEFORE CHECKING ON HER? No need to bring the groceries in now. IF ANYTHING HAPPENED TO HER, HE WOULD ALWAYS FEEL HE WAS TO BLAME. Thus distraught, he closed and locked her door and went back to the office to await a call from Paula.

The news, when it came, was not good. Pneumonia! Paula would not consider leaving Mrs. Strickland alone. "NO", she told Pete. She would stay right there with Mrs. Strickland as long as she was unconscious. NO, he should not come to the hospital. Mrs. Strickland could not have company .

"I'll come pick you up, then. You don't have a way to get home."

"Pete, I'm staying right here. I told the ambulance driver that she is my grandmother. They will let me stay. I JUST KNOW THEY WILL! I'll call you later." He started to say something, but heard nothing but the dial tone. With nothing else to do, his thoughts turned to the ones who were closest to Mrs. Strickland. His hand seemed unable to dial Kelly's number, and she was the one he most wanted to call. Instead, he called Frank.

The Emergency Ward at Baylor was a whirlwind of activity. The curtained area, where they had moved Mrs. Strickland, was barely large enough for the Doctor and Nurse to complete their work on the patient. Although Paula pleaded with them, she was ordered to wait in the reception room like everyone else. They would call her when the patient was ready to be taken to a hospital room. Not even the tears moved them from that order. Paula found a seat and sat.

An hour later, she was invited to go with the medic who would roll her grandmother to the hospital room. After tucking the patient into her bed, the understanding attendant showed Paula to the snack bar in the visitor's lounge.

"Honey, help yourself to coffee and juice and whatever else you like at this bar. I notice someone has brought doughnuts by today."

"Is it OK if I take it to her room? I'm not going to leave her."

"Yes, you can do that, but she will be monitored and using oxygen, and she will be wearing an I V tube. I think you would rather be at home than here." Seeing Paula's rejection of that statement, the nurse continued.

"However, you will find that lounge chair in her room will stretch itself into a neat sleeper if you are determined to stay. I'll unfold the lounge chair. You'll find a blanket and pillow in the closet. Why don't you have that coffee and roll while we get our patient ready for the night. Take your time. She's in room three thirty three just down that hall on the right.

Paula followed that advice and suddenly realized it helped. They had finished with the attachment of tubes and hose and placed an oxygen mask to Mrs. Strickkland's face when she tiptoed in and stood at the side of the bed to watch the unconscious woman being given the crucial treatment.

Watching each thing the nurses did for the patient's comfort and recovery became indelible schooling for the younger woman. The sincerity of her questions was rewarded with uncommon consideration.

"Yes, of course you may hold her hand whenever we are not working on her. In fact, it is possible that she might feel your presence. Love has a way of healing, a way we do not understand.

"You may as well eat this. She is getting her food intravenously, and the tray is automatic." She looked at Paula's perplexed frown.

"You started to say something, didn't you? What's on your mind?"

"Well, I was thinking about her being hooked up to that tube. It seems like maybe it is putting new life into her. Is it?"

In a way, that's true, but the patient's WILL plays a part in that procedure, too. Your grandmother's responses suggest that she is a strong person, and that can go a long way toward recovery."

"Well, I wish I had some new life pumped into me," Paula sighed.

"What else is on your mind?"

"Why does she have to have those tubes in her nose? And why does she have to keep breathing in and out of that one thing?"

"That is oxygen that will keep her lungs from filling with fluid. It helps to get your grandmother well again. It is important to keep her lungs clear while we treat her other symptoms. You would make a good nurse, Paula."

"Do you have to have training to do that?"

"Yes, but that should not be a problem for you at your age.

"But I didn't finish high school. How could I get into training?"

"Honey, you get yourself down to the Junior college and ask at the administration office what you would have to take to quality for training. Why not? If you want to do this kind of work, there is certainly room in this field."

"Really? *But I didn't finish school." She repeated. "Wouldn't that keep me out?" Paula's face registered her fear even as it foretold her hope.*

"Yes, REALLY. You would make a good member of the medical field, but you really should go home, don't you think? Denying your own physical needs would go against all of the rules for being a good nurse."

Paula's eyes filled with tears. "I just can't go off and leave her. I'll sit here in the corner and I won't be in the way. Will that be all right? PLEASE?"

"Is she your grandmother?" The night nurse studied the younger woman's face for an affirmative answer.

"Sort of." Paula hedged.

"All right, but it is going to be a tiresome night. I can assure you of that. She is being checked every few minutes, and she should not be engaged in general conversation. Do you still want to stay?"

"Yes I do. Thank you, thank you!"

Pete had argued with himself ever since the ambulance took his friend away. At last he called the hospital and asked about the condition of Mrs. Strickland. Then he asked if the young lady friend was still there and if she needed transportation. It was difficult for him to believe that Paula was insisting on spending the night.

"Oh, yes," the nurse who answered assured him. "And you are not the only one who has called to check on both the patient and her guest. In fact, a Miss Richardson has requested that her name be put on the list to be called in case of emergency. Mrs. Strickland is a fortunate lady to have such caring friends."

"Thank you." Pete replaced the telephone. Then he slammed his fist down on the desk top. Another demerit for 'Pete, the fool!' He had offered too little too late. He owed more to Mrs. Ida Mae Strickland than he ever admitted. Why was he so resentful of her constant willingness to help him? A college BA degree certainly did not do much for his human relationships. Instead of demeaning her all these years, why hadn't he been grateful?

On the third day the fever broke, and Mrs. Strickland recognized Paula. The loving reunion was Christmas gift for the caregivers in the hospital. Now, for the first time, Paula was convinced to return home, and an ambulance driver was willing to take her. She could not prevent the tears that fell as she said good bye. Mrs. Strickland smiled weakly and, just as weakly, attempted to repeat a Bible verse. She could quote but little.

" To everything there is a season. A time to be born, and a time to die, a time to weep and a time to laugh. Go home now. Now is a time to be happy, Paula."

Kelly was in the hall when Paula closed the door to Mrs. Strickland's room.

"I called to check on our friend, and they told me you are ready to go home; so here I am here to take you. Just let me have a brief peep at our friend. We've been missing you, Paula. You wait right here, please, and let me look in on her. I'll just be a minute."

Inside the room, the patient's hand lifted in recognition of her guest.

Kelly shook her head and patted the hand that was free of needles and tubes.

"No, I didn't come to visit. I just wanted to see you and know you are all right. I am taking Paula home, and I will look after her until you get there. You have become like a mother to that girl, and she is behaving like a daughter to you. What a wonderful thing to have said of you!"

"Is it Christmas yet? I wanted to get some things to go under my tree for everyone. I have sort of lost count of the date and time."

"No, it is several days before Christmas. Besides, you need to let the rest of us tend to that business. Use your energy in getting back that vibrant personality we miss so much. Right this minute, you should be resting. I will leave you in good hands and take Paula to lunch before going home. I will also be here to give you a lift home when they say you can go. May I do that?"

The answer was slow in coming, but gratitude showed in her eyes.

"Thank you, Miss Richardson."

"Miss Richardson did not make that offer. KELLY did." She gently brushed the patient's forehead and winked before walking away.

As she returned to the hall, she noticed that the past several days had left marks of their tedium on Paula. Kelly put her arms about the girl's shoulders and pulled her close.

"Thanks for coming for me, Kelly. I know Mrs. Strickland loved seeing you. You know, I have been thinking a lot the past couple of days. Do you think I am too old to take nurse's training? It is something I think I would like to do. What do you think of the idea?"

"For you or for me?" Kelly laughed." Personally, I can't generate much enthusiasm for bedpans and thermometers, but relieving pain does seem to be a workable part of your makeup. Certainly you are not too old to pursue that, or anything else, as a vocation. You might even want to ask one of the nurses at the hospital what they think."

"I did that, and one of them said I should ask the Junior College what I would need. I guess it is pretty expensive, though, and there is something else, too, Kelly, I am thinking of moving to a cheaper apartment."

"Would this thinking have anything to do with your association with the other Peas?"

"Maybe. I don't fit in like I thought I would, and besides, I don't know how much longer they will keep paying me my salary. And I keep thinking about what that preacher was saying about being responsible for what we are making of our lives. I don't like what I am making. Do you know what I mean, Kelly?"

"I think I do. I also believe something else, too." Noting Paula's questioning eyes, she continued. "There are many, many things far worse than death. I believe every person can change the direction she is going IF she has a sincere desire to do so. And I believe that our thoughts and our actions determine what goes on in our lives. Every genuine wish we make, and for every thought, if they are sincere and issued for the right reasons, are likely to be fulfilled. There is a reaction that takes place in our lives when we set our goals on a worthy path. That is a law, Paula, known as Action and Reaction. It is one of life's unfailing laws, and it operates in everybody.

"To me, that means if I choose the wrong goals for my life, I will become the misfit that must live with my decisions. God doesn't slap us with the verdict. We do it to ourselves. We have all heard that as a man thinketh, so is he. That is this unfailing law. If we admire an activity and want to be part of it, we are setting up the way to get there. Do you see what I mean?"

"Well, yes, when you put it that way. Is that what the preacher meant when he said 'THINK ON THESE THINGS?" That's scary, isn't it?"

"Only if you choose to think of it as scary. What is more frightening is the payment we earn by holding onto the wrong values and beliefs and deeds." Kelly studied Paula's face for a moment before continuing. "Let's stop at Denny's and have a bite to eat before we go home. You probably haven't eaten today, and this would give us more time to talk." Without waiting for a reply, Kelly turned into the driveway of that destination.

"I'm not dressed very well, Kelly."

"You look great to me, Kiddo. Let's go in. Okay?"

Inside they waited at the entrance to be shown to a table. Once seated, Kelly opened her purse and, unnoticed, turned on a small tape recorder. What came forward was unexpected.

"Kelly, you like Pete a lot, don't you?"

"Well, he's nice. I like him, yes. Why do you ask? Don't you like him?"

"He gets too bossy, but I guess I like him. But YOU like him A LOT, don't you?"

"Hey, I didn't know we came in here to talk about me and whether I like somebody."

"Okay. I can tell you do, though You like him a lot, and that is all right, too." Paula seemed satisfied.

"Paula, what has this to do with you and what you want to do with your life?"

"Nothing. I just thought if you ever get married, you wouldn't live in your own apartment any longer, and I wouldn't get to see you as often. That's all."

"I see. You are thinking of getting another apartment and you are a little afraid to step out on your own. Right? And you want to pursue the idea of nursing, but you feel you need a friend to guide you, someone to talk to about it. Correct? And this past weekend did nothing to improve your lack of self-confidence? Honey, how did you ever get into such a messy life? How old are you, Paula?"

"I am fifteen, but you won't tell Pete, will you?"

"Don't worry. I won't get you in trouble with Pete, but how did you get into this situation?"

Paula's eyes blinked, but the tears were already rolling down her cheeks. Their waitress stood waiting with order pad in her hands. Kelly nodded as she returned both menus to her and turned her attention to her upset guest.

"Two specials, please."

She gave Paula ample time to compose herself before saying anything more.

When their orders were placed in front of them, Kelly took a bite and chewed slowly, watching for Paula's control to return. At last Paula looked up and made an attempt to respond to Kelly's earlier question."I don't know," she offered. "Some way I just got caught up in it, and I'd give anything to undo it."

"Well, I think you have gone a long way toward undoing it, Paula. Your aid to Mrs. Strickland is a great start, anyway. You have made a very good friend in her."

"Yes, but when I left, she said 'to everyone there is a time to die', and I'm afraid she will."

"Of course she will, dear. So will you and so will I and Pete and everyone else living at the apartments. In a way, we start dying the day we are born, and every day we live is one day closer to the time we will die. That is the beautiful thing about life, we all have a given amount of time to become our very best selves and to overcome earlier misdeeds. Right this minute I am seeing a young woman who is thinking of various paths she might take. She is hoping to choose the path that will take her to her highest level. Does that make sense?"

"Right now it does, Kelly, but I just hope I don't let Patti and Pris talk me out of it." Her face recorded her fears and hopelessness.

"Paula, would you like to stay in my apartment with me for a few days?"

"Could I? Oh, Kelly, that would be wonderful. I wouldn't even have to listen to them trying to get me to work with them. But I wouldn't want to be a bother to you."

"Then why don't we go home and start moving? But make sure this is what you want to do. I would be very disappointed in you if it turned out that you wanted to get back with those girls or that you weren't serious about pulling yourself up!

Kelly, I PROMISE you I won't do that. I really, REALLY want OUT! But what about Pete and the rent and the deposit? I don't even have enough to pay my rent this month."

"I hope Pete will go along with us, especially if he can believe you are sincere. What about the two guys who live next door to you? Do they have any kind of hold on you?"

"They have already collected their commission from me; so I don't think they can stop me."

"Paula, do you mean they were taking a cut on what you made by entertaining men?"

"Yes. I thought you knew."

"Who all is involved in the ring, Paula? Who is the head of it and what kind of arrangement do you have with them?"

Kelly's eyes did not waver from the girl's face as she listened to the sordid story of drugs and debt and threats that pulled her down into the mire of a wide ranged activity. What was supposed to have been fun and popularity and security after having run away from home had evolved into slavery.

"What about your parents, Paula? Where are they, and is Paula your real name?

"My dad left my mom and me when I was five. Mom left me with neighbors while she went out to work every day. Then she started bringing men home with her, and sometimes they drank so much that I had to take over for myself. We didn't have any relatives, or at least I never knew of any. Then one day I was sitting on the doorstep trying to figure out what to do, and this guy came up and asked me to go with him to get a bite to eat, and when he paid for our lunch, he put a twenty dollar bill in my pocket and said he'd like for me to meet his son.

'The next day he came by and introduced me to one of the guys that lives in the apartment next to me now. Then I met Pam and Pris, and they wanted me to move in with them. They were making good money, and they invited me to join them. So I did. My mother didn't know I was around, anyway, even when she was a little sober. My name was Lula-Bell, and I changed it to Paula so I could be one of the three Peas."

Kelly was conscious of a knot in her throat. It was difficult to swallow. She was certain now. Her suspicions were correct. The two ad specialists were but collectors for Manny La Banta's prostitution ring, and they did the bookkeeping, collecting and pay-off for the suave Mister La Banta. PETE NEWMAN WAS NOT INVOLVED.

Kelly closed her eyes and shook her head. "Oh, Paula, what an awful, awful trap you have stepped into. Why don't you go to the ladies' room and wash the tears off your face while I pay our check?"

*"Where is it ?"*Kelly nodded in the direction. As soon as Paula was out of sight, Kelly opened her bag and turned the recorder off as she pulled out her cell phone. She dialed a number and spoke softly into it.

"Standby Code thirty-two plus three. We should be in my place in thirty minutes.

"I picked up some juicy steaks for dinner. I trust you won't mind that I have a friend staying with me for the next several days. She will help me prepare dinner, so don't have anyone bring anything to my apartment tonight. You'll love these steaks. They are PRIME BEEF. They cost a pretty penny, but you will agree they are worth it. See you soon." She dropped the cell phone into her large, softer-than-silk, leather bag. She smiled as Paula returned to the table.

"Okay, Room mate, let's roll, shall we?" She led the way to the cashier's desk.

Once more Kelly opened her bag, this time to bring out a twenty dollar bill to hand to the cashier. She dropped the change into her bag and put her arm around the girl and steered her back to the car.

"Thank you, Kelly. I enjoyed that. Someday I am going to be able to repay you for all the times you have been so good to me; I just KNOW I will."

" Okay, I'm going to hold you to that," Kelly's answer brought a smile to the girl's face. The smile lingered in her voice as she added:

"Oh, Kelly, I don't know what I would do without you. I never had anyone I could trust or..."

"Hold it right there! If you and I are going to be living under the same roof, we're going to have to start off on equal terms. You are not taxing me by accepting my offer of a place to stay just now, and you don't owe me apologies, nor undue gratitude. Let's start off with honesty and friendship without blowing it up into an emotional event. I know you meant it when you said 'thank you'. That is all you need to say, and I only need to say, 'you're welcome'. Fair enough?"

"Yes, thank you," Paula giggled.

"You're welcome," Kelly giggled back. Arm in arm they laughed their way back to the car.

"You must be eager to take a bath and change clothes after this length of time. When we get to the apartments, you can go right up to my unit and crawl into the tub." Her outstretched hand held a door key.

I have another key, Paula; so you can go directly to my apartment. Don't open the door to anyone. NOT TO ANYONE! Do you understand? Go up the side stairs so you won't be seen. I'll park the car and be right up. Now SCOOT!" She stopped close to the side stairway and motioned for Paula to go.

She lost no time in driving around to the back of the building where she parked in her usual space and walked at her usual pace into the courtyard where Frank Fisher was taking pictures of the flowers he had been tending.

"Hello, Miss Richardson. How are you this afternoon?"

"I am very well, thank you. It is amazing how you can keep flowers blooming in this weather. No wonder you take pictures so you can prove that you did it." Kelly walked to where Frank was standing. She bent down and cradled a geranium blossom in her hand.

"Why, you cheater," she teased as she discovered the flower was artificial. Frank bent over the same flower and picked up the small tape reel she had dropped in the plant pot.

"I didn't want us to have a winter- bare area so I improvised. Sorry if I cheated."

Kelly continued on her way to the stairs, and looked back at Frank.

"I won't tell anyone if you don't." She chided. Frank grinned and waved her on. He took the steps two at a time and disappeared around the corner toward his place. Kelly was more nonchalant as she climbed the stairs to hers. "It's me, kiddo," she called as she entered and locked the door behind herself.

" Just stay where you are, and I'll bring you a robe to slip into. Take your time, honey, and use some of my herbal bath beads. You'll love them." Kelly took a chair near the front window where she could monitor events. It was not long before the action commenced.

Within an hour the entire area was surrounded by uniformed police and several plain-clothes officers. Residents in units number thirty-two, thirty-three thirty-four and five were summoned by persistent knocking and calls to 'open up'. When there was no answer, the doors were forced open, and for the following hour the thorough searching produced two males and two females, each hand cuffed and led between two armed guards to the police cars below. Two of the officers carried sacks of confiscated evidence.

Not until the abrasive shouts were no longer heard did the other residents open their doors or venture to look from their windows. When quiet was restored, Pete's telephone began to ring. He was as much in the dark as the callers were.

"No, I do not know what the trouble is. I assume it was something connected with last week end, but I do not know." Over and over he was forced to repeat those words. When the caller was Kelly Richardson, though, he was gentler in his answers.

"Pete, can you come up? "

"Of course. I'll be right up.' She was watching for him and held the door open. Expecting her to voice the same question the others had asked, he was prepared with the same response he had given to the other phone callers.

"Sit down, Pete. I think you need to know that Paula was not a part of that uproar. I picked her up at the hospital, and she did not want to go back to her apartment; and I had her come up here so she could bathe and get some rest."

"Where is she now?"

"In the bedroom. No one saw her come in here, and I promised her she could stay with me for awhile. We need to get her things from her apartment, and I wanted to ask you how much it will take to get her out of her lease. She wants to go into nurse's training, and she is scared to death of seeing any of her roommates or the two men neighbors. What do you think we can do?" Kelly's words tumbled over each other on their way to his ears.

"WE?"

"Well, I can't do it all by myself." Kelly's eyes looked directly into his.

"How did you get mixed up in this mess, Kelly?"

"I walked in on purpose. I watched that girl taking care of Mrs. Strickland and saw how she continued to stay with her. I did not just happen to go to the hospital today. I went when I called and was told that the patient was better and that Paula was being urged to go home. On the way home I stopped for us to have breakfast and it was then that I learned that she was a run-away who had been lured into the ring that has been operating here in this complex and how she hates it and how frightened she is. That is how I became involved. But my question was WHAT CAN WE DO ABOUT HER CONTRACT?" She tossed the ball into his court.

"And you are SURE I will destroy the lease agreement and overlook the deposit, huh? That is my part of this 'WE?" Pete's raised eyebrows held a challenge.

"Something like that, I guess." Her smiling challenge over ruled his.

"You're a beautiful woman, Kelly, and your body language would have most men falling at your feet, BUT I'M NOT ONE OF THEM! GET YOUR AVAILABLE MANNY LaBANTA TO FINANCE YOUR FANTASIES!" Pete stood up and took a step toward the door. "COUNT ME OUT!"

"Well, maybe I will have to ask him to help, but he is not, and never has been, MY AVAILABLE MANNY LaBanta! He happens to be general manager of the club where I work, and he was very generous in furnishing the gadgets for the pool party. You were impressed by that gesture, but you refuse to do what you easily could to assist a young woman to reach a goal that will enable her to rise above her unhealthy environment.

"Don't trouble yourself, Peter Newman. She can stay with me, and all I will ask of you is to help get her things from her apartment and to tell me how much it will cost to release her from her rental agreement."They heard a sob from the adjoining room. Both looked up as Paula came through the door. Kelly was on her feet in an instant, protectively pulling the girl into her arms.

"Let me go, Kelly! I don't want to be the cause of trouble between you two. I can handle my life myself, and I don't need another job or school or anything else." Again she tried to be free of Kelly's arms Pete opened his mouth to speak, but nothing emerged. He swallowed and tried once more, his arms flinging about like windmill fans.

"I'm sorry, Paula. Let's start over. Suppose I agree with Kelly's suggestion. What is the next step in this tableau?" He was looking at Paula and speaking to Kelly.

"We move her things in here with me and get the apartment cleaned up so it can be rented again.

"And what if the other girls return and demand to know what we are doing?"

"Oh, we won't have to worry about that. They won't be coming back. Neither will the two fellows who were their neighbors." Kelly tilted her head and smiled ever so innocently at Pete.

"Somehow I feel like I didn't get a full plate when the food was passed around. Is there a key to the missing element in this play?"

"Possibly, but you wouldn't want to spoil the punch line before seeing all of the movie, would you?"

"Kelly, I swore the last time I bought a Lottery ticket that I would never buy another. I guess I was wrong. So when do we start this move that is going to cost the heck out of my bank account and play hop scotch with my bookkeeping?"

Kelly shook her head when Paula started to voice another rejection.

"Why not right now so we can beat the crowd returning from work. There's no need to upset everyone's appetite before dinner, is there?"

It was a silent triangle of persons who stood at this moment and looked at each other. Paula's tear streaked face and eyes, which betrayed her past several days without personal care, hovered like a bird readying itself for flight. Pete was feeling like an oaf. He desperately wanted to undo the hurt he had imposed on the young woman, His was the look of a man who regretted his most recent past while not knowing how to replace the hurt to both women with some sort of compromise on his part.

Kelly's eyes did not waver from Pete's face. Her arm was still, although loosely, around the girl, indicating her willingness to take on all adversaries. The silence in the room was broken only by the heavy breathing of the three.

Chapter IX

All's well that ends well; still the finis is the crown.
Shakespeare

"Let's go!" Pete was shaking his head in disbelief as he followed Kelly to Paula's apartment.

Normally, Frank could be seen about the place at almost any hour, but today he was the invisible man. If Pete had thought of asking him to assist in this move, the thought was painted in the wrong colors. However, the transition required very little time. Paula's closet held a minimum of clothing. Personal items were shamefully non-existent, and only the bed showed signs of a past weekend struggle. Pete went to the utility room and returned with the vacuum sweeper. Kelly had vanished with Paula's possessions, including a note written to the girl by Mrs. Strickland.

What puzzled him was an item in the upper corner of the bedroom wall. It looked like a camera secured with Velcro or similar substance. He didn't remember having seen it before. He was sure it had been a late addition to the unit. The ugliness of the possible answer sickened him.

After sweeping, Pete returned the machine to the storeroom. Because he had not been officially notified of the status of the two men whom the Police had taken, he did not enter those units. Had his dad faced situations such as this? Surely Kelly would shed more light on this matter now that he had complied with her request. As he headed for her door, he saw Frank checking on those artificial flowers of his. He looked up and waved at Pete and then bent to his earlier task. Playing with those fake flowers was a dumb thing for a grown man to be doing in this weather, he thought. In fact, lately, everything was strange.

The food Kelly ordered from the caterer was delivered shortly after Pete reached her door.

"Please don't fuss about this. I thought it would be a good way for you and Paula and me to do some visiting. You don't mind, do you? And please stop looking like you have a head-shaking disease"

"I'm beginning to think I may have," he countered.

Following the lunch and visit with Paula, Pete returned to his apartment to check his telephone messages. What a strange month it had been! The summer had gone so well that he had assumed his problems were behind him. Now his complacency was being unraveled. Although his financial situation had crossed over into the green area, this latest episode promised to upset that balance. Worse than that was the possibility of losing his friend, Mrs. Strickland. What a naive bumpkin he had been, thinking his only problem was finding what was in those jellybeans!

Here it was nearly Christmas time, and he had no idea what was expected of him. There had always been his mother or the matron at the Boarding School who handled those things. Even Mrs. Strickland had prompted him about duties at times when he forgot.

Kelly Richardson seemed to have an answer for everything. What if he went back to her apartment and see what she would say if she were in his boots. He discarded that idea a couple of times before finding himself half way up the stairs to her door.

Kelly had a great deal to say. First, she had made a few calls and had found that there was an immense need for nurses in this and other areas. "According to the answer I received from my call to the Dallas Chapter of the Texas Nurses Association, about fifteen per cent of Registered Nursing positions are vacant in the Dallas-Fort Worth area, and the need is growing greater all the time." These she rapidly enumerated to Pete.

"Pediatrics areas are in dire need of radiology technicians; medical technologists, dietary aides, and psychiatric nurses lead the list, but Paula, seems to prefer geriatrics as her field."

Application blanks and brochures will be mailed at once.

"But her age of fifteen is going to be a difficult hurdle, I'm afraid, unless she can enter as an understudy until she is at least seventeen. I thought, perhaps, if she stayed with me and ate with me, that maybe you could help with the additional expenses. I have enough clothes to share for the full term of her training." Kelly was exuberant in her forecasts.

"STOP IT, KELLY! I understand your haste in helping the girl, but there is a little matter of what the law may require of her when this trial comes up, and.." He was not allowed to finish his statement as Kelly continued.

"That's just it, Pete. The trial isn't just a little matter. It is a real chunk of importance that she be enrolled and with proper guardianship for the Judge to use in his disposition of the case. Can you think of a more suitable gift at Christmas time than the opportunity for a secure future to one who right now is grasping at a last straw? If you can help a little bit with expenses, I'll request that I be made guardian for the rest of her teen years. Mrs. Strickland will probably want to help, too."

"Please don't make such a request of Mrs. Strickland. She should not be burdened with this problem."

"That is just the point, Pete. IT IS NOT A PROBLEM. IT IS ELIMINATING A PROBLEM."

"Why is it I always get the feeling I was left out when sound reasoning was distributed? What logical explanation have you figured out as a back up for that statement?"

"Pete, you make me think you don't trust me at all."

"Oh, come on, Kelly. Of course I trust you. It's just that you take me down the lane a bit fast. Okeh. Suppose I agree. Then what?"

"Then you'll do it? Oh, THANK YOU, PETE!" Kelly crossed the room and kissed him on the cheek.

Before Pete could intervene to remind Kelly that she was LaBanta's girl, she added:

"This is something you will NEVER regret, Pete. It is not often one has the opportunity to literally save another human being, and that is exactly what your aid will be doing. I just can't thank you enough. You are a dear; really you are."

"Cut it out, Kelly!" Embarrassed by her exuberance, he stood up and headed for home.

The following day Kelly received the telephone call that sent her scurrying to bring home the oldest resident of the complex. Knowing that Paula would insist upon going with her, she asked her to make a pot of tea and make the room presentable for some good news to follow.

At the hospital there was paper work to be dealt with. Kelly dealt with it. There were instructions for the care of the patient. Kelly accepted the list and listened as they were explained to her. Thus she saw to the official release and the nurse tucked her passenger into the car. On the way, she called Pete to report and to ask that he recruit Frank to assist the lady up the stairs and into the apartment that was warm and welcoming with fresh flowers and her favorite young friend, Paula.

"Of course I will, Kelly. Does she need to be carried up or can she walk with our assistance?

"She thinks she can make it on her own, but I think she will need support. Do you think Frank will help?"

"I am sure he will be glad to help in this or anywhere else we need him He is a good man, Kelly." Pete's vexation was dissolved with this turn of events.

"Yes, he is, or, at least I believe he is." Kelly noted the change.

Personal news travels fast, and many of the tenants were bundled up and waiting outside to welcome the old lady back to their midst. One young man was conspicuous by his absence. He had taken a ride to the hospital to pick up his wife and newly born son. The date was December sixteen..

Chary Reasoner joined the courtyard crowd and quite suddenly began singing JOY TO THE WORLD. Once again, he found himself leading a host of voices .As the melody rolled from one into another and another, the new mother and father arrived with their babe swaddled in a blanket. As they made their way around the pool, they were followed by the group's lusty voices singing 'IT CAME UPON A MIDNIGHT CLEAR.'

As though the song called forth the group cooperation, two of the men flanked the new mother and assisted her up the steps to the babe's new home. Although several of the women rushed to relieve the man of the bundle he was carrying, their help was unneeded, unwanted, and unaccepted. The new father would carry his child with no help. It was obvious that he had been searching biblical names in search of the right one for his son.

"We'll call him David because he truly is 'WELL BELOVED.' With that announcement, he pointed his toes in the direction of young David's new home.

"He looks too little to fight off a giant," Chary called after their departure.

No one noticed when Pete and Frank wandered toward the side entrance and quietly welcomed Mrs. Strickland and gave her their strength to climb the steps. Alas, again the grapevine news whispered that Mrs. Strickland had arrived. With hardly a pause in their jubilant welcome of young David, the body of welcomers flocked to her doorway. And, again, the welcoming voices gave vent to the fervent joy bursting from each. 'JOY TO THE WORLD,' they sang with believable strength.

Once inside, Mrs. Strickland had eyes for but one person. Paula, wearing a silk pajama set, was all she sought.

"Oh, how good it is to be home and to see everybody. Paula, I do believe you have grown even prettier since I last saw you. Come here, child, and let me give you a hug."

"I'm glad you are here, too, Mrs. Strickland. Things just aren't the same without you."

"Don't you mean without my crabby nature?" She laughed and looked around her living room. Until now she had not seen the tree standing in the corner awaiting her notice of its many lights and trimmings. Colorful wrappings on the several boxes and packages spoke the language of loving friends who had contrived to make this occasion special. Her delighted squeal surprised even its author.

"Oh, what is this? Who did all of this? Oh, my, and I didn't get to do any shopping for everybody. How can I deserve this.?"

"Don't you remember hearing the preacher saying 'In as much as you have done it unto one of the least of these, you have done it unto me?"

"I certainly do remember that, and I also remember hearing him say 'Do unto others as you would have them DO UNTO YOU, and, then, He said 'IT IS BETTER TO GIVE THAN TO RECEIVE'. And since I wouldn't have you be concerned about my lack of Christmas gifts to all of you, I am going to give you the BETTER part of that statement. You can't have these back. It would be to deprive you of the blessing of your gifts."

Laughter and applause accompanied her attempt to override the glint of happiness. "Hey, look, every one! She is back with us, and they didn't remove her fun nature. LET'S GET OUT OF HERE AND LET THIS LADY GET TO USED TOO BEING AT HOME. Only after they left did she glance around the room until her eyes landed on her beloved genealogy chart. It was exactly where she had left it.

Christmas Eve created memories that would last a lifetime for all who dwelled here. The beauty of its spirit continued into the next morning. No frolicking marred the quiet simplicity of this post card scene. In the distance could be heard the bells of the little church. In the street there appeared the annual sight of boys and sleds. Pete Newman stood marveling at the happiness within him. Nothing had changed; and EVERYTHING had changed.

He could almost hear again the melodious voice of Chary's spontaneous singing. Might that be the reason for this euphoria? Or was it the sight of Paula's face as she realized she could have help in reclaiming her future? It went beyond that and intermixed with witnessing Mrs. Strickland's gratification at being home with those she loved. No, it was all of those things, and, most of all, the feeling seemed to have stemmed from Kelly's kiss on his cheek. Pete's fingers touched the spot.

'Yes', he concluded. 'It was all of those things, including the birth of young David.

Even so, was it possible that SPIRIT, any SPIRIT, could be an entity in itself? Was that the secret the clergy was describing to the group which recently had invaded his church? Pete's recall of that evening was crystal clear. As the minister told the old story to them, he mentioned several times that GOD IS LOVE, and that Love is all-powerful. We didn't discuss it very much, but we all HEARD it. Could it be that we have all been touched by this Spirit of Love? He needed to think about these things, maybe for a long, long time.

What an unbelievable number of events had come into his life! This thinking left no room for amazement that the frocked figure entering the courtyard was one and the same man who had welcomed them into his church. It simply completed the picture that had been forming in his mind.

"Merry Christmas, Reverend. Are you lost or are you looking for an apartment?"

Pete's chuckle accompanied his outstretched hand.

"Neither at the moment, but the garden area is certainly appealing." His hand gripped Pete's. "I believe you shelter one of my Parishioners, Mrs. Ida Mae Strickland. Am I correct?"

"Yes, she lives in number twenty; Shall I call her to say you are here?"

"No, don't go to that trouble. She called earlier today to ask me to drop by." Aren't you one of the caroler's who favored us with your songs recently?" At Pete's nod, he added, "Your visit was noteworthy to our entire congregation. And, the gentleman with the magnificent tenor voice is living here, also, I believe?"

"Oh, you mean Charles Reasoner? Yes, he lives in that unit you just passed, although I didn't realize his voice rated that distinguished description," Pete offered.

"It does, indeed, sir. He has one of the most precise and trained voices I have listened to in a long while. I hope to interest him in joining our choir. If he is in, I shall stop in after I visit Mrs. Strickland. If you happen to see him, before I return, will you please tell him I shall stop in for a short visit?"

"I will be happy to do that. By the way, I think we didn.t sufficiently thank you for your hospitality when we imposed on you to add your blessing and inspiration to our spontaneous visit. It was a wonderful entree to this Season. We all thank you."

"Well, come back again. The door is open every Sunday, and we will consider your presence a belated payment for the season." The parson's friendly laugh demonstrated his ability to match Pete's humor; then he turned and, giving a hasty wave of departure, strode toward the steps leading to number twenty.

Pete grinned and shook his head and headed to Chary's door.

Chary opened the door at the first knock, but his landlord simply stood eyeing him and moving his head up and down, a broad grin signifying the presence of a mystery.

"Okay. What is it? Why are you wearing that silly grin?"

"It beats me", Pete said as he scratched his head and produced an even broader grin. "What can that preacher see in you that I can't see? He wants to visit with you and get you to sing a song for him." Pete was not worried about the mangled message. "He will be here shortly. Do you think you should practice or something before he gets here?"

Chary studied Pete's face for some retraction, but none came. Instead, Pete asked more seriously.

"Where did you learn to sing like you do?"

"I take it you are asking whether I ever took voice lessons, yes? Well, the answer is, YES, I DID. My father tried to program me for opera, and my interest was in hymns and spiritual music. Our constant disagreement in that field was the lever that pried us apart. He would not attend, nor allow me to attend, my mother's church, and he thought my church songs were preventing me from climbing the ladder he had placed for me. Is that what you wanted to know?" Chary's irritation crept into his voice.

"I'm just kidding, Buddy," Pete apologized. The Reverend is quite interested in your talent and will be here to tell you so as soon as he has visited with Mrs. Strickland. I hope you aren't offended. As a matter of fact, I am one of your fans, too."

No. That's okay. I am so hurt by my father's attitude toward spiritual music that I get overly protective of it. Sorry about that! I guess that is why I responded to the seasonal music the way I did during our snowy trek to the church. It just feels good to let that beautiful story roll out. I've felt better since doing so. This doesn't embarrass you, I hope?"

"Not in the least, Chary. In fact, I teased you about it because I was rather awed when the Reverend asked me to let you know he would like to stop by and visit with you. He is with Mrs. Strickland right now, but I'm sure he will be here shortly. I congratulate you, Buddy. You have your head screwed on exactly right. I wish I could say the same thing about mine. The Reverend must be endowed with a special sensitivity. He recognized sincerity and genius when he heard it"

"He would have to be extra sensitive to have been so gracious to us wandering peasants invading his sanctuary as we did. How is our friend in number twenty?"

"Mrs. Strickland? She is well enough to ask the Reverend to visit HER. She has been going to his little church for a long time. On most Sundays the same taxi driver stops at the same time to pick her up for service. Someone always brings her back here. I had no idea until just recently that it was that little church that she attended. Much of the time someone takes her to lunch just after service."

"Isn't she asking for company too soon after being as sick as she was?"

"Chary, that lady is so revived that I think she is trying to regain those lost days. Asking for a visit from the Clergy, or, maybe I should say 'DEMANDING A VISIT', goes to prove her built-in-stamina. She is okay."

"I cannot imagine why he wants to see me." Chary's disbelief was sincere. He could not get the Parson's visit off his mind, and he had not over-long to wait for his answer. The Reverend, having concluded his visit with Mrs. Strickland, came down the steps and started directly to Chary's door. He stopped when he recognized another member of his parish.

Gene Seals, coming down the back stairway with a grin spread across his face, charged across the walkway to offer a happy greeting.

"What brings you out slumming today," he inquired of the frocked figure.

"I'm out proselytizing, Gene. Don't tell me you live here?"

"I can tell you haven't studied the current addresses of your flock, Rev. I've been here for a little while now."

"Then you know our Mrs. Strickland who lives here, too, I suppose?"

"Sure, I do. She's the number one reason everybody here is so chummy, or hadn't you noticed? I'm on my way to rescue a customer whose car is playing dead today. I'm ushering Sunday morning, so I know I'll see you there. Right?"

The jocularity ended their encounter, and the parson turned his thoughts and his steps to Charles Reasoner's place. Pete remembered some book work needing his attention and nodded to the reverend as he left them.

As promised, the visit was short. The offer was made; the offer was accepted, and the awed computer expert forced himself to walk calmly to his neighbor's door as the reverend departed. Pete held the door open for him.

"Can you believe THAT, Pete? He wants ME to be in his choir. ME! Oh, I wish my father could know this. It's like a miracle, Pete. He plans a Springtime presentation, and he asked me to render solos throughout.

"Well, why don't you let your father know about it/"

"He wouldn't care. He'd probably laugh in my face."

"Think about it, Chary. He will more than likely be so happy to know where you are that he will jump at the chance to see and hear you. This just might be the opportunity you have both waited for. Go for it, man!" Pete clapped his hand onto the excited man's shoulder and watched the glow of happiness spread over his face.

"Maybe you are right. I wonder if Mrs. Strickland will come to hear the choir."

"It would surprise me very much if she did not, and I am sure there will be several other of your friends attending when they learn of this. I certainly plan to be there."

"Oooh Man.!" Chary grew more excited by the minute. Pete grinned and left him to dream.

Mrs. Strickland was not surprised at the news. The Reverend had confided in his oldest Parishioner when he visited her. Her effervescence was a match for Chary's elation.

She would, she told Kelly, host a tea for his friends who attended the choir production. Already she was making mental notes for a lavish party.

"Do you think you should be doing anything that strenuous at this time? You are still weak from your pneumonia." Kelly attempted the impossible task of advising the lady.

"Nonsense. It is this kind of activity that keeps me alive and going! Besides, I am sure Paula will help even if you won't."

"You KNOW I will help you any way I can, Mrs. Strickland, and Paula has her heart set on the studies she hopes to pass before she can enter Nurses Training, but I feel certain she will do whatever she can. Since we don't have a date for the Recital at this time, why don't we wait about planning the tea.?"

"I KNOW WHEN IT IS GOING TO BE! It will be Springtime, and Mr. Fisher will have the courtyard beautiful with his flowers. It will be pretty enough for a wedding even though there is no one in this complex ready to cooperate in that department." Pursing her lips into a tight knot, Mrs. Strickland indicated that the conversation had just ended.

Kelly, recognizing the finality of the subject, bit her lip to hide the smile which threatened to cover her face. Mrs. Strickland was indeed a remarkable woman. Her words left no doubt that she was well aware of the budding interest between Pete and Kelly and that she would like to see the ultimate outcome escalate to her imagined picture.

Charles Reasoner worked and re-worked the wording on his invitations. Practice for the big event would be each Sunday evening until the target date of May fifteen. It had been established that MR. CHARLES REASONER WOULD BE THE SOLOIST, and, as such, he felt that using his full name would be most appropriate. His computer expertise was immensely helpful in creating the impressive notes. It was, furthermore, most imperative that he give his best efforts to the company for which he worked. No longer did he dwell on the past life and his feeling of guilt at what might have been.

CHARLES REASONER was a gainfully employed computer analyst whose golden voice was sought by the Clergy. That very knowledge infused his entire being with a dignity over-riding his usual foolishness. He insisted upon driving Mrs. Strickland to church on Sundays. At her insistence that she take him to lunch following the morning services, he considered himself duly thanked for such accommodation.

After work-hours during the week, Mr. Reasoner kept to himself. If Pete missed his pseudo brother's daily communications, he hid it. His time was spread amid other requirements. Little by little the apartments underwent needed repairs. New carpets were laid; The smell of fresh paint became a subliminal selling point to prospective tenants answering the ads. Filters were replaced and crisp, new drapes enhanced the windows.

Frank's casual greetings were usually a welcome part of the day, but not on this day. There were beginning to be far too many unnecessary conversations pertaining to the recent events, and Pete had more important things on his mind. He did not care to indulge in gossip, if that was what one could call Frank's lurid curiosity, and, if the questions came from a more serious interest, Pete had no desire to join nor to contribute information, nor even to answer a question.

His agreement to help with Paula's struggles dictated the need to update the apartments, including their appearance and reputation. Now he was noticing that to keep a ninety per cent occupancy, the eye appeal was as important as physical amenities. At any rate, the place was more than paying its own way, and Pete was pleased. Instead of bankrupting him, it seemed that his income had doubled since he had followed Kelly's lead in helping Paula.

Yes, all things were going well, he had to admit that the suggestions which came from Kelly Richardson had been responsible for much of the improvement. He really ought to take her out for a nice dinner, some expensive place with atmosphere. But where? The more he thought about it, the more he realized that he'd have to ask her advice about where she would like to go.

Seeing Frank advancing, Pete felt disinclined to listen to the man's casual greeting.

CHAPTER X

A human being is not, in any proper sense,
A human being till he is educated.
H. Mann

"Is Paula coming along okay? I seldom see her anymore. Has she ever discussed what happened up in her place?" Frank seemed overly interested in that affair.

"She is doing very well. I didn't question her about the situation, though. She does plan to go through with training to become a nurse."

"Good for her, Pete, she seems like a decent girl that just got her directions mixed."

Pete's response was coated with frost.

"That's how I see it, too. I need to try again to reach the number you gave me; so if you will excuse me, I'll do that now."

"Go right ahead. I transplanted a little pot of ivy for Mrs. Strickland, and I'll take that up to her. She is a sterling character if I ever saw one." Frank said to the empty space where Pete had stood. His hand rubbed across the back of his neck as he turned around.

Questions about membership were swiftly answered to Pete's satisfaction.

"Send an application, please" was his immediate request. Meetings held on the first Thursday of each month offered no deterrent. The next meeting fell in the coming week, Pete vowed to be present.

His application and check were in the mail the day after he received the forms. Thursday dawned clear and with mild temperature. Pete accepted this as an omen of good things to come. Provided with the new roster of members, both owners and service providers for the apartments, he discovered why many of his dad's earlier friends were members of this respected organization. Somehow, he had always thought this to be sort of a union for owners and managers of renting houses. NOT SO, he decided now.

At the first meeting Pete learned from a long time member that there was an unspoken method of communication between managers of these businesses. The speaker was a well-known member of the Bar Association and a County Servant. Pete's interest grew and his attendance became a promised reality. When he learned that his advertisements were permitted to include his affiliation with the prestigious group, his impression escalated. This was what he needed!

Supplied with his pad of lease forms, Pete headed for home with a renewed interest in the future. From now on, he promised himself, things would be better protected and more carefully managed. It was then that he remembered Chary's question about how he kept the books for the apartments. He would like to learn the ins and outs of the computer programs, and he seriously hoped Chary might be able to guide him through the program.

On the other hand, with Chary's current interest in music and the practice it involved, it would be inconsiderate of him to request such help. Aloud he stated.

"I'll see how these record forms and leases turn out before I tackle something new." There are enough tangled events that require my time and attention right now.He had not solved the problem of the jellybeans; nor of Frank's questionable actions, and his own agreement to help with Paula's future would keep his available time at a minimum. Not until he reached his parking area, did he convince himself to slow down.

He pitched the packet of leases and other data onto the desk as soon as he entered his unit. There were several calls on his answering machine, all of which needed a bit of attention.

He made a note to call Kevin Keystone immediately after work hours. He could understand why they wanted to change their apartment for one on the lower floor; climbing the stairs was beginning to be difficult for his wife. Pete did a quick mental excursion of the whole complex. There were two which might serve the purpose. They could use some refurbishing, too; so he could schedule the painter and carpet layer as soon as the Keystones indicated their choice. Number forty two needed a plumber, and the thermostat in unit fifty was not working well. He'd better check all of them.

Of course, there was no complaint from Kelly Richardson's place. Pete grinned at the thought. Nothing could go amiss as long as she was head of her locale. IT WOULDN'T DARE. What a woman! He wished...., but, on the other hand...

For the next few hours, because it was the bottom line of keeping his finances balanced, Pete's concentration was aimed at taking care of the apartment's requirements. Might as well replace the air conditioning and heating filters while he was tending the other needs, he decided. Saving a few steps here and there could make a big difference in his energy level at the end of the day.

One other thing could be handled while he was in the storage room for filters. He should take a quick inventory of filters, pool supplies and replacement items. What he had not counted on, however, was the jumbled shelves where he normally kept such items at hand. Putting those in order would take some of the time he needed for the tenant's complaints to be corrected.

"Wow!" Pete said it aloud. Once it got started, life itself could pick up speed beyond reasonable fulfillment. He pulled down a box of filters and, without looking back, closed and locked the storage room door. "If I'm not careful, I'm going to have to have a written agenda for every day."

"Hey, Pete! I made it! I made it!" Paula was waving a paper as she ran toward him. Pete waited. This is BOUND to be good news.

"Whatever it is, it's bound to be good news! What is it?"

Paula skidded to a stop in front of him. She was too out of breath to continue; so she handed him the paper to read. Even so, she began again before he could decipher it.

"The G.E.D., Pete! My equivalency test! I passed it! I have that high school graduation behind me. I can start classes now. I am going to be a nurse!"

"Paula, that really is great news. What did Kelly say about it?"

"I haven't told her yet. I saw you out here, and I just had to tell you before I went on upstairs." She took the paper from Pete's hand and ran toward the stairs. He stood watching her joyous ascent. He was, at this moment, witnessing genuine happiness. He wiped his eyes and swallowed. Kelly was right! He would never regret the little he had been able to do to help produce this sight.

Still feeling the girl's excitement, Pete picked up the box of filters he had dropped when she approached. Come to think about it, taking an interest in the tenants is a true pleasure. Pete began humming a happy lilt. The 'Smiley' face on the temperature gauge had nothing to do with the feeling of warmth today. A wide grin spread across his face.

"Wouldn't it be wonderful if a person could turn this kind of happiness on simply by helping another. Wow! It almost makes me want to go looking for a person with a need I can fill. Whoa, Pete. Try to solve all of those needs of Peter Newman before taking on the whole world"

Pete continued his way to the upper floor and changed the filters in a few units before entertaining a new thought. He might possibly need some help to run this place. It was beginning to be a drain on his time He'd give the thought some attention, he laughed, soon as he could find the time to do so.

He had never before realized how much energy it took to manage the sixty units. Things always seemed to operate on their own momentum.

With one hundred per cent occupancy, the financial corner did very well, but requirements of maintenance devoured the time one set aside for proper bookkeeping and taxes. No wonder so many owners employed persons to discharge these duties.

Yes, he should do something, and relying on Mrs. Strickland for everything was not a viable answer. More than ever, he began to chide himself for his poor handling of their relationship. Instead of her owing him an apology, he most certainly owed her one. Watching her growing friendship with Paula pulled at the heartstrings. There was something of a grandmother feel to that picture.

CHAPTER XI

There is no happiness for him who oppresses and persecutes;
There can be no repose for him. For the sighs of the unfortunate
Cry for vengeance to heaven.
Sophocles

It was more like a period than a comma; more like a question mark than a question, and more startling than an exclamation point. The morning news announcement was shocking even as it offered reasonable support to logical thinking.

'MANNY LABANTA'S DEATH RULED SUICIDE. CITY WIDE DRUG STING NETS BIG AND LITTLE FISH'

'Tony LaBanta, Manager of the Colonial Country Club of this city, was found dead in his hotel suite at five A.M. Friday morning. His gun, with one missing bullet, was found near his body. LaBanta has been long considered by the FDA to be a leader in the prostitution crime of this city. In a simultaneous effort, fifteen houses of prostitution were raided, and enough evidence obtained for Grand Jury action. This is thought to be..."

Pete scanned and then re-read the story. He dropped the paper when his phone rang. As though connected to a central control, the announcement set off a flurry of telephone calls. Many were directed to Pete's number. By the time his mind accepted the news item and he assured the several callers that he was as much in the dark as were they, his thoughts fastened on Kelly. Did she know yet? Would she cope well with it? She had not called him. Should he call her? He did not wait for a response from his mentor before hastening to her apartment.

He had been right in his evaluation of Manny LaBanta. The man was the low scum Pete had always thought him to be. Was it possible that the trouble in four of his units was fed by this same source? With every question which presented itself to his racing mind, the tighter his stomach felt. His face was ashen when Kelly opened the door to his knock.

"Are you all right, Kelly?"

She had been made aware of the news by a co-worker, and was dressed to go wherever she was needed. Though serious, she was nonetheless in total command of her actions.

"Kelly, can I help?"

"Yes, Pete, you can. Please keep an eye on Paula and be sure no strangers are allowed in to see her. I will be fine, but I must go to the club to keep things as smooth as possible. Please stay close to Paula and to Mrs. Strickland. I cannot vouch for their safety if the wrong parties decide to pay them a call."

"But why Mrs. Strickland? She couldn't possibly be mixed up in this!"

"That's true, Pete, but someone could know more than they are saying, and they could cause harm to either or both parties."

"But WHY?"

"Because they may think Paula has talked about the organization, and that she could be controlled by seeing the lady tortured."

"Over my dead body!" Pete rose to his full height, his face flushed in his fury.

"Let's not play heroics, Pete. This is serious, and caution is the better part of valor just now. Please keep cool. I promise to tell you the whole story when I return." Kelly took a deep breath and continued.

" These killers are not intimidated by conscience nor legalities. Back off and let the officers involved be the ones to call the shots.

"Where do you come into the picture, Kelly?"

"I guess you deserve the right to know. I am an agent with the Drug and Firearms Division of our government, Pete. Frank and I are partners on this case, and we each moved here to keep tabs on the setup that was a part of the expansion of the ring. We had to know whether management was involved, or whether they even knew what was going on under their noses."

"Are you telling me that I have been under suspicion all this time?"

"No, not YOU, but the complex was, and it was our job to find and apprehend the culprits. This is why I helped to pull Paula out of it. She is just one more victim they work on to run this ugly business of exploiting young women. I have called in with stomach complaints for the past week in order to stick around to keep an eye on her. Surely you must have known I was up to more than merely befriending a wayward teenager, didn't you?" Kelly's eyes telegraphed her plea.

"I knew SOMETHING was going on, but it didn't occur to me that you were a part of anything like this. I need to know something, Kelly. Were those jellybeans mixed up in any of this mess?"

"In a way, yes. There were only two beans laced with a truth serum, and they were meant for you and Chary. We had to know whether you two were in on the La Banta business. Your pills were laced with a truth drug far less addictive than the actual ones Manny had planned for this little party. He had hoped to learn whether the two of you could be added to his growing family of users and solicitors. I'm sorry you both had bad reactions. Frank and I searched for a long time before we found plain candy jellybeans which we could substitute for the ones La Banta intended for us to use. Those were the real stuff and would have done great damage had we used them." Kelly stopped for a breath before continuing.

"But why in the world would anyone suspect me? Or Chary, for that matter."

" Manny had the five working upstairs, and, seemingly, you did nothing to stop them; so he thought you might be open to the idea of expanding the business here. I went along long enough to learn that you and Chary knew nothing about it." Kelly's smile showed her glad reaction to what had been learned. "We saved as evidence the ones he had given to me to use. The ones you and Chary took were mild in comparison to those we were supposed to be using. "Frank kept them and the ones we had left. They were given to the officers along with the real ones La Banta had supplied. All of them are considered as evidence. Manny figured on the real ones enticing the managers to want more and to sell for him. We thought we could learn who was at the head of this ring by giving a mere sample of the real thing. Manny wanted to enslave the entire complex membership."

"What a sorted mess for you to be engaged in, Kelly. It's horrible!" Pete spread his hands as though to empty them of such a thought.

"Does knowing about my part in it make any difference in our friendship?"

"Well, no, not that. But I guess I hoped we might be headed toward being more than just friends. I guess I feel like...well, ...come here, Kelly." Pete pulled her into his arms and did what he wanted to do from the first day he saw her. When he released her, they stood looking at one another in a new way. Finally, Pete uttered a weak moan.

"Oh Man!" It sounded like a final amen. Life can be very confusing! He would have liked to take her into his arms again, but she backed away.

"I have to get going. You WILL look after our two lady friends, won't you?"

"Yes. Of course I will. Do you expect any trouble at the club? Should someone go with you?"

"No, to both questions, Pete. But I do need to get over there NOW." She stood on tiptoe and kissed him on the tip of his nose, and left him standing on the balcony by her door.

"Don't forget where we left off." Kelly grinned playfully at him and walked away. As she left, a bonny laugh assaulted Pete's ears.

"Would you care for something cool to drink?" Chary, of course.

"That wouldn't be a bad idea. Are you buying?"

"You bet. Come on into my abode. I want to find out what you have that I don't have and why it has never been seen before today." Chary's humor was genuine good fellowship. Pete's feet followed the teasing voice from the first floor.

"No comment. How are your practice sessions going?" he countered.

"Pete, I wish I could tell you what a wonderful feeling it is to be a part of such a great group. I can hardly wait from one session to the next. It's like a miracle."

"The more I think about things we have learned recently, the more I can see that things might not be 'LIKE A MIRACLE' but possibly BE miracles. Look how long you have had the desire to sing these songs. And think how many hours you spent practicing and training your voice. And then, Chary, can't you hear the words the preacher used when he read 'As a man thinketh in his heart, so is he.'

Doesn't it make sense to you that your success is inevitable? Everyone living here is looking forward to attending the big event when you are featured in a recital. Let's just accept it all as a genuine miracle."

"Thank you, Pete." Chary was still awed "What do you think of the news in the paper this morning?

"Enough to know I'd rather discuss something else. Okay?"

"You got it! That's the second good idea you've had in the last five minutes. Do you mind if I ask how Kelly is taking the news?"

"Well, that was her boss, after all. Of course she is upset, but she's handling it. Anything else?"

"I guess not. I'll see you later."

Thus the gruesome details of Manny LaBanta's demise were denied unnecessary discussion, but an inevitable pall replaced the apartment's recent gaiety. The ugliness of their close touch with such horrors faded the brilliance of their good times. Paula's disassociation with the Three Peas gave the tenants incentive to open their hearts and doors in friendship.

News of her GED test, and the upcoming classes for Nurse's Training, became the opening for conversations during the ensuing weeks.

"Paula, you even walk like a different person. We're so proud of you! You are like a member of the family to everyone of us. You're going to become the most sought after nurse in this state; you just remember that!" Everyone had a word of encouragement.

It was true that the girl walked with a new and confident step. No longer did her head dip forward in an attitude of shame and fear. Gone were the careless items of her attire. The harshness of her former dress and manner was replaced by Kelly's offerings. Now her appearance showcased the determination and belief in her future. Paula was headed for her highest potential, and it was visible in every step she took. Her comings and goings were dictated by the hours of her classes and her deliberate study periods. Her one friend was young Fran Seals, and, where the two girls were to be seen, Pete was acutely aware of that special aura of teen happiness.

"Kelly," he said one afternoon, "Have you noticed how different Paula is these days? It looks like you have been a great influence on her. She even looks different, and Fran's grandfather tells me he is noticing the same kind of a change in Fran. It is unbelievable."

"Why so? Everybody responds to the confidence others place in them. Until you started seeing her as a human worthy of being helped, she accepted herself as unworthy and useless. Without a goal and someone to assist in reaching it, she really was heading for a spot in the annals of the untouchables.

"Pete, your help has meant more to her than you can possibly imagine." Kelly's eyes held gratitude and pride in her landlord. If she hoped for a greater show of trust from him, it did not show. And, if Peter Newman wanted at that moment to embrace her, he managed to hide it.

Chapter XII

Barkis is willin''
Charles Dickens

Spring came early that year. Shortly after the crocus bloomed, the Bradford Pear trees began to bud. Soon the grackles were loosing their occasional raucous cries, and a freshness enveloped the air. A million grass blades sprang to life. The calendar proclaimed the date, March one, and the winds proclaimed their right to dominate the city. Tornadoes were reported in varying parts of the Lone Star State.

Pete Newman was perspiring in his apartment. He needed air. Pulling a blanket from his bed, he took it and a magazine outside and spread it on the dead, grassy area by the pool and lay down on it. He blamed spring fever for the lethargy that threatened to overwhelm him. He hadn't felt in top shape for some time and had decided, this morning, to catch up on his rest and reading. He had read but a few pages of the "Modern Apartment Management" magazine when he fell asleep. When, finally, he awakened, the shade had wandered away from him, leaving him in the accidental sun bath. Somewhat befuddled, he rose to his feet and became aware of an inexplicable weakness and numbness in his left leg. Forgetting the blanket and his magazine, Pete staggered toward his apartment. His hands, like ice, shook uncontrollably. After some time, his mind began to clear and his breathing became more regular. He sat on the concrete bench to allow his senses time to recover from whatever had numbed them. The weakness remained.

At last he stood and resumed his arduous trek along the shaded walk to his apartment. He felt he had never before walked so far to attain such little distance. When this long walk ended, he was in his apartment, but he did not stop the agonizing journey until he reached the telephone and dialed 911. That was all he remembered. He had no idea how long it took the paramedics to answer his call, actually only eleven minutes. He was unconscious as they loaded him into the waiting ambulance.

Kelly parked her car just as the patient was being loaded. When she recognized Pete, she insisted upon accompanying him. Assuming that she was the patient's wife, the paramedics made no objection. They worked as though she was not there, talking by phone to the ER and describing vital signs. The trip was mere minutes in route. When the door of the ambulance opened, instant hands rolled the gurney out, extended it's legs, and rushed the patient into the building. Kelly followed to the emergency entrance and was directed to wait in the waiting room.

She called Chary from the courtesy phone and received only a message from his answering machine. He was out for the moment but would return the call. She was dialing Frank's number when a hand touched her shoulder. Turning, she was relieved to see Chary and Frank.

Forty-three minutes dragged by. It was like waiting for an announcement from God. The doctor emerged from the ER, pulling the rubber gloves over his hands as he came. Kelly heard his report seemingly coming from a great distance.

"He will be all right, but we are admitting him. He should have no company just now. We will keep him sedated for some time. He is dehydrated and in a stressful condition. I suggest you go home and we will call you when he is awake."

Reluctantly, with the encouragement of Frank and Chary, Kelly agreed to go. It was obvious that Chary's mind was fastened onto some unrelated thought. He was with them, but his mind had wandered afar. He folded his long legs as he squeezed into the back seat of Frank's car, but he said not a word until they were well on their way home.

"Mrs. Strickland does keep a key to the office, doesn't she?' he asked Kelly.

"Yes, I know she does. She always watches the place for Pete and even rents an apartment when he is not around."

"I'm just thinking out loud, but it seems to me that Pete could save himself a lot of trouble and time if he would get a computer to handle his books and all kinds of records."

"Chary," Kelly was shaking her head and smiling. "Can you imagine Pete Newman sitting still long enough to learn to use a computer?"

"YES. I can imagine it! I see it all the time in classes. Once a person sees the possibilities, they are hooked. Pete is working too hard, and ..." his voice trailed off as the car stopped in the parking lot. Unwinding his legs to exit, he added, "I'm going to see Mrs. Strickland right now. I have an extra computer in my apartment. It's one I use in classes sometime or when another one goes on the blink." He was on his way up the stairway before Frank and Kelly made it into the garden area.

Pete's dreams were on-going events. He was protecting Mrs. Strickland from gangland thugs. He was on one knee asking Kelly to be his wife; He was listening to Chary singing at his recital, he was watching as Paula slightly inclined her head to receive the coveted cap. He was distantly aware of the needles drawing blood from his arm. Only when the wrapping of the blood pressure monitor awakened him did he realize where he was or why he was there.

Back in the conscious world, it would be Chary who manned the office. With Mrs. Strickland's guidance, he and Frank brought a folding banquet table from the storage room and set it under the picture window. The computer parts were lined up along an adjacent wall.

"That doesn't look much like a desk," Kelly laughed.

Not to be discouraged, Chary countered, "I don't look much like an apartment owner, either, but I am acting like one."

"It looks good to me," Mrs. S defended. "What comes next?"

"The computer itself. That's that tower looking thing with all those slots and odd looking buttons and vents." He lifted the gray hulk onto its appointed space.

"That's it? Why don't you set it on the end of the table?"

"Because that space has to be dedicated to the printer...which we don't have yet."

"Will it operate without a printer?"

Chary ignored the question for a moment, then continued his statement, saying, " Because I don't have an extra one. Pete can look at what he stores, though, any time he wants to open a file drawer to read it. All he has to do is take it out of the file drawer and show it on the monitor, this little TV screen here." Chary patted the monitor and tilted it for comfortable viewing. 'But it has to have power to show the movie. It has to be connected to the computer and also to the control panel which we call the keyboard" His hands demonstrated each item as he described it.

"This is a mouse, but not one you want to catch in a trap. He will behave quite well staying on his little pad to serve your needs by pointing out your location when using the keyboard to put a message on the monitor." Chary picked up the plug end of the mouse cord and attached it to the back of the computer tower.

"This long piece has all of the plug-in places along with this switch that turns the computer off and on. Sometimes a problem can be solved by making sure all connections are in the right place." He laughed and added, "If that doesn't work, you call me."

A program has already been installed in this machine. It is what we use in classes because most users have a need for the information it handles. Mrs. Strickland, I am going to show you how to file the records on each tenant living here. You will use the available leases to glean that information. No one else needs to have it. This is going to become an indispensable record keeper of great value to Pete, and I have a feeling YOU are going to have fun doing it. You DO type, don't you?"

"I can handle that. When do I start?"

"Well, we have to hook the phone to the computer and then attach the computer to the phone connection. The computer will work without a printer, but it won't print out a message without a printer. The computer work can still go forward. Right now we are setting up for using the computer to manage and store vital records.

"We have to have a keyboard to relay our data to the computer so it can sort and store the info in the correct file drawers hidden in that tower we call a computer. Are you getting the picture?"

Mrs. Strickland nodded. "You explain it so even I can understand it, Chary. That is wonderful. But I still have a question. Why don't we have a printer?"

"Because I don't have a extra one. Pete can look at what he stores, though, anytime he wants to open a file drawer and read it. He can read it anytime just by taking it out of the file drawer and showing it on the monitor" He would have continued, but Mrs. Strickland had more to say.

"How much does a good printer cost?"

"Around four hundred dollars, but to continue."

"I want to buy a printer. How long will it take to get one? Or can you use the one on your computer and let me buy another for you?"

"Let me go get mine, and we'll see about the other one. Is that all right?" Chary was out the door and well on his way to unhooking his printer to satisfy Mrs. Strickland's wishes. In less than twenty minutes, he had it installed and was ready to continue.

"The monitor is this little TV screen here." Chary patted the monitor and tilted it for comfortable viewing. "But so it can have power to act as the movie show, it has to be connected to the computer and also to the control panel we call the keyboard." His hands were demonstrating every movement as he talked. Picking up the smaller part of the set, contented. "This is a mouse but NOT one you want to catch in a trap. He will be very happy staying on his little pad to serve your needs in pointing out your location when using the keyboard to put a message on the monitor." Chary picked up plug end of the mouse cord and attached it to the back of the computer tower. The telephone broke into the lesson.

"Chary, this is Gene. If you are the acting manager, you should know the answer. I just saw a little mouse running for cover in my bathroom. Do we call an exterminator, or what?"

"Gene, that subject didn't come up in my management briefing, but Mrs. Strickland will know. Just a minute." He turned from the phone and asked "Does anyone know what to do about a little mouse taking over Gene's Bathroom?" The question caused immediate laughter in the office. Realizing the improbability of such a question coming at the time he was talking about the mouse, Chary attempted to quit laughing and give a reasonable interpretation.

"No one here seems to be able to answer your question, Gene. Do you have any suggestions?", he asked the caller. At this question, those in the office dropped all pretense of withholding their uncontrolled mirth. Not knowing anything else to do, Gene made a final try. "Well, yes, I think I do. I know these apartments have a 'NO PETS' rule, but I keep an orange cat at my shop, and he is a good mouser. Anyone object if I bring him over as a loan? If not, I'm going to the shop right now and get him."

"Why don't you do that, Gene? Is this a male or a female cat?"

"I've never examined him, but he doesn't show a preference in whether the mice are male or female. His name is Max. I assume that is a masculine name. Anybody have an aversion that name?" Laughter was once more unloosed, and the line went dead. Chary, still chuckling, reached for a long switch box and continued with the lesson.

"This long piece with all the plug-in places and the switch, is where you turn the computer off and on. If you try it and find it doesn't come on, check to see that all parts are correctly connected. Sometimes a problem can be corrected by making sure of all connections." He laughed and added "and if that doesn't work, you call me.

"As I said, a program has already been installed in this machine. It is the one used in classes because most users have a need for the type information it handles. Mrs. Strickland, are you ready? And I have a feeling YOU are going to have fun doing this."

"What do I do first?"

While Chary instructed Mrs. S, Frank, who had been giving full time to the physical needs of the complex, stopped in to report on that state of affairs.

"Number forty called to say her disposal was stopped up, and I didn't know what to do about that except call a plumber. Then she told me that Pete always uses the handle of a broom to free the blades for action." He wagged his head in astonishment. "And I did not know, before taking on my unassigned duties, that people get really teed off when someone else pulls their laundry out of the machines and pokes their own in. If it weren't for all of us having our own key to the laundry room, I wouldn't have believed anyone in this complex could be that rude."

"Oh, my goodness!" Mrs. Strickland cried out. "I was so interested in this computer that I forgot. That was MY laundry. Oh, I hope I haven't caused someone to be inconvenienced. My! I'm going right now to tend to that." She was ready to go in a second.

Frank laughed and stopped her. "I'm kidding," he offered. "I saw you put your linens in early this morning. Being the good manager that I am, I long ago took them out and folded them. When you are ready to leave your classroom, I'll even carry them up for you. Just say when."

Having had his fun, he continued with his animated report.

Chapter XIII

None preaches better than the ant, and he says nothing.
Ben Franklin

"Then, would you believe that number thirty two ran the vacuum sweeper too close to the draperies and got one caught in the vacuum sweeper roller? I had an awful time unwinding all that fabric. I'm afraid Pete is going to have to buy new drapes.

Life's activities continued. Concerned questions and brief answers passed between the ones coming or going for the next few days. Paula's classes waited while she and Kelly attended the hearing against the Peas and the two Ad men. At their initial appearance the judge noted that each of the accused was listed as indigent and therefore in need of an appointed attorney, a matter which was quickly handled. He also noted that, when the Records of past misdemeanors were brought to his attention, the evidence was overwhelmingly against them. A trial date was set for later, and all of the accused were remanded to be held. Paula could not look at her former room mates. Her eyes misted.

Tony LaBanta would not be a threat to anyone again. His death assured it. When the judge suggested that, due to Paula's adolescence, she might be made a ward of the court, a solemn quiet brushed the room. All eyes were glued on the Judge who was acutely aware of the prevailing attitude. He smiled and said directly to Paula:

"Young lady, I am placing you in the care of Ms. Kelly Richardson during the term of your training to become a nurse. I wish you well, and I trust you realize how lucky you are to have the kind of friends who showed up here today. I think I do not need to remind you that your fate might easily have gone another way" He rose and added." This court is adjourned"

Clapping filled the empty space where quiet had prevailed. Paula turned to Kelly and threw her arms around her. Kelly made no attempt to stem the spate of tears that coursed like rivers down her cheeks. The partial release of the strain of the past weeks broke through the will power that had held her together. Looking around at the friends with cheeks as damp as her own, Kelly smiled and let the tears continue.

Paula would be expected to appear at the grand jury hearing, but only as a witness. One of the charges brought against the older participants in this criminal hearing was that of coercing a child under the age of seventeen to indulge in prostitution and possession of drugs for sale.

"Can we go home now?" Paula was eager.

"Not just yet, honey; there is a bit of paper work and instruction first." Kelly took advantage of the lull to call Chary, wishing as she did so that it could have been Pete she was calling.

Topping the day's good news was the release of Peter Newman. His hospital stay was short and the diagnosis held an admonition to supply his system with more nutritious food. He had allowed himself to become anemic, and his blood pressure indicated a need to relax. Medication couldn't do the job alone; he must help. He listened and he agreed. He knew, too, that the task before him was more than a one man job.

Pete hoped it would be Kelly who rescued him from the odors and sounds of the hospital. Instead, it was Frank, and disappointment clouded the convalescent's face.

"Do not worry, sir. I have orders from her majesty to deliver you directly to her abode," Frank bantered.

"Does it show that plainly?"

"Admit it, man. You are a GONER, Sure it shows, you lucky son-of-a-gun." Frank was still smiling as he parked the car and opened the door for Pete who insisted on stopping at his apartment before going to Number Twenty. There was an important matter to be addressed first. He went directly to the bathroom and opened the cabinet by the sink and withdrew his tooth brush and razor. Frank said not a word about the computer which awaited Pete's first trip back to the office. While Pete transformed the hospital ennui, Frank continued to scan the area hoping to see Kelly and Paula arrive. He was acutely aware that Chary and Mrs. Strickland were working as fast as accuracy allowed. Hopefully, the computer installation might be complete before Pete was introduced to his new office routine.

Even as he watched in anxious anticipation, Kelly and Paula came into view. They headed directly to Pete's door and entered just as Pete closed the bathroom door behind himself. Quite suddenly the room was overtaken by three eager speakers, all with a different story to tell. With the lowering of voices, there remained but one thing to be attended. Chary rapped on Pete's door and ceremoniously extended Mrs. Strickland's invitation for each one to come to the office. From there, it was history. Pete Newman became the newest member of the computer generation.

December ushered in the new year's calendars, and January was afforded its due respect. At mid month Gene Seals took the necessary time to go with his granddaughter to knock on every door in the complex. Girl Scout cookies would be ready for delivery in February, and every troop was vying for the prize for selling the greatest number. Gene went with the girl as she rapped on each door, but he stepped a few feet back as the door was opened by his neighbor. The girl must make a sale by her own winning personality and sales ability.

The few who did not order cookies were wished a pleasant year. Gene was proud of his 'genes' accepting a 'no sale' with the same quality of good will as with those who ordered.

"Thank you for your order. It will be delivered in February. If it is delayed, just let my grandfather know." Her eyes went toward Gene who was waiting a few feet away. His wave acknowledged his role in the sale.

February brought snow. Early on the morning designated as delivery day, a large truck backed up to the entrance way of the apartment complex. The driver, with the aid of Gene Seals and his excited granddaughter, made the rounds to deposit an order at every door, even to the doors which had not produced a sale. Grandfather was making sure there would be no doubt about the winner of this year's sales.

Max, in an air of guardianship, accompanied the girl as she delivered the cookies. Although his normal avoidance of adults was well understood by the tenants, it was easy to decipher the message his homage intended. Max acknowledged the teen ager as his only friend until, finally, Paula was allowed to rub his orange covering. Girls, only, he liked.

"If I didn't know there will always be warmer days ahead, I would leave here," Pete complained.

"And where would you go?" Ida Mae Strickland queried from her side of the computer set-up. You'd just miss the homecoming of the Purple Martins the last of this month, and you just might end up somewhere the volcanoes or hurricanes ruled. So where would you rather be right this minute?"

Pete pulled himself out of the comfortable desk chair in front of the computer and, rubbed the back of his neck before answering.

"I still can't get over how you and Chary managed to get this computer thing going while I was away. And I certainly cannot understand your interest in it. I think you have grown younger instead of older, but what I really can't see is WHY DIDN'T I get into this method of handling the apartment business long ago? It has opened my eyes to many things I didn't even know existed. "Mrs. Strickland, you really are a remarkable woman. I owe you"

"Nonsense! Anybody around here could see the computer can do the work of several people. Chary happened to think of doing this while you were away, and I just wanted to learn something about the computers, so Chary's loan of a set did a lot for several of us. It's Chary you owe, not me."

"And what is this about you buying a printer? I owe for that."

"Peter Newman, I've been telling you for most of your life that there is as much grace in accepting a gift as there is in giving one. I don't want to hear anymore about it."

Chapter XIV

There is in every true woman's heart a spark of heavenly fire
Which lies dormant in the broad daylight of prosperity;
But which kindles up, and beams and blazes in the dark night of adversity.
Washington Irving.

Even though the calendar over his desk affirmed it was Saturday, March 15, it seemed to Pete to be Sunday The courtyard was empty of all except a stray cat in search of food.

"Cat, you had better be gone before Max comes around the corner or you will be escorted out of this area." The time was 9:07 and on any other day, the tenants would have been stirring. Pete's gaze fell upon Mrs. Strickland's front window.

"Funny her light should be the only one on," he thought. Then he saw that her porch light was also on. He picked up the phone and dialed her apartment. No answer. Then he dialed Chary's number.

"Hullo," came the voice of one attempting to sound fully awake.

"Hey man, I didn't mean to wake you up!" Pete ad-libbed as an opening statement. "Are you ready for coffee? Come on over, I just brewed a pot," he lied; knowing he would have the coffee ready by the time his friend arrived..

"Be right there," Chary said, "just as soon as I've showered."

Pete left the front door ajar. Chary didn't knock He pushed the door open and playfully announced.

"I'm here. Feed me!"

Pete motioned toward Mrs. Strickland's lights. "It's unusual to see her porch light on at this hour."

"Yes it is. I guess she is getting a little bit forgetful these days." Chary surmised.

"Let's run up there and check. Okeh? She didn't answer her phone when I called a little bit ago". Pete was a little concerned. Chary thought there was probably nothing wrong, but they should go and wish her a happy day, anyway. As they left Pete's place, they noticed their neighbor making his way to the courtyard area.

"Good morning, Frank. What brings you out at this hour?" Pete kicked at leaves the gusty breezes were swirling down the walkway.

"I didn't sleep much last night. The wind sounds like 'Mariah', doesn't it? I'll have these leaves cleaned up in a bit, but the way it's blowing..." His voice trailed off into nothing. "Sorry I overslept today" he apologized. "I'll have this task finished soon."

"There's no rush" Pete offered. "No one else is up and about."

As they approached number 20, Pete could feel the hair rising on his arms.

“Something is wrong, Chary,” he uttered.

“I feel it, too, Pete, something is not right.” At the partly-opened shades in the window, they could see Mrs. Strickland sitting at her desk with her back to the window.

“She must be getting deaf as well as forgetful.”

“Right.” Pete pressed the doorbell, waited, and then knocked. Silence followed. He inserted his master key and opened the door and wailed “OH, MY GOD! NO!

Mrs. Strickland sat in front of the desk, lifeless, with paper work in front of her. Instantly at her side, it was Chary who had presence of mind to call nine-one-one. Pete was stunned.

“Take it easy, Pete! Go home and get control. I’ll take care of this end for you.”

With Pete away from the scene, Chary organized his thoughts. First things first. Number one: tell Kelly. Number two, call the Reverend.

“Where is Pete?” Kelly asked.

“I sent him to his apartment, Kelly. He is horribly upset. See what you can do, will you?”

Kelly was on her way before Chary finished speaking. She opened the unlocked door to Pete’s apartment and quietly entered.

Pete was sitting on the edge of his bed, his forehead buried in his right hand, his elbows on his knees, his eyes, focused far beneath the floor, seeing nothing. He lifted his head as she sat down by his side and pulled his head onto her shoulder.

“Oh, Pete! I’M SO SORRY!”

A bit startled at hearing a voice, Pete shook his head.

“She’s gone! Kelly, SHE’S GONE!” The dam was not strong enough to hold back the devastating emotion. Waves of remorsefulness and sorrow rocked his body to and fro.

For a long time, Kelly held him and sat beside him. Finally, Pete stood and walked to the window. Little knots of people stood together sharing their shock at this current loss. Chary and Frank were standing near a pile of leaves that Frank had been raking from the walk Sadness hung over the grieving tenants like smoke in a valley. They did not leave the area until watching their much loved friend being taken from the last place she had called home!

Through the gated entrance to the courtyard came the Pastor of their little church. Chary had called him at once. He made his way toward the waiting group and put his hand on Chary’s shoulder.

“I’m sorry”, he said. “Where is Mr. Newman?”

Chary’s forefinger flipped in the direction of Pete’s place to point him to the door.

The Reverend did not wait for an invitation to enter. He tapped on the door with the knuckles of his right hand as he pushed it open and stepped inside.

"I'm terribly sorry," he said and laid his hand on Pete's shoulder Pete nodded in response.

Kelly nodded to the Reverend and stepped into the kitchen to afford some privacy. There, on the counter were several sacks of groceries. Obviously he had been to the store, and, just obviously, he had not put away any of them. She began at once to remove the frozen items for the freezer; then she began to store the non perishable foods. That finished, she went back to the living room and would have left had Pete not motioned for her to stay.

"Pete, I know our friend would want you to approve the plans she made for her final resting place. Would you prefer to talk in her place or in your office?

Pete looked at Kelly.

"Why don't you go into your office, Pete. Paula should be coming in from her classes very soon, and she is going to need me with her." She looked at him with a tenderness that gave him the strength he needed .

"Thank you, Kelly." Pete nodded toward the office door and led his guest inside.

Once seated, a brief case was opened and a sheaf of papers was lifted out. Pete dropped his head onto his chest. How could he go through with this, even with the Pastor making it as easy as possible? He swallowed. Then he reached for his handkerchief and blew his nose. He swallowed again and looked up.

"Sorry", he excused himself.

"Don't be ashamed or afraid to cry, Pete. God is aware of the pain you are suffering. And so, I believe, is Mrs. Strickland. As a matter of fact, that is why she asked me quite some months ago to be the bearer of some good news she had for you whenever the time came for her departure. She KNEW she was going, Pete, and she was ready for the trip."

"Good news? How can this be good news?"

"She was a better friend than you knew. Not only did she claim you as her only heir, leaving her entire worldly goods to you with but one stipulation. She talked with me at great length, Pete. She was especially concerned about the care and training of young Paula. It is her last wish that you use whatever is needed to assure the girl's training and future welfare. She requested a simple service, with no flowery platitudes. She insisted that Mr. Reasoner be in charge of the music and hoped the residents of the apartments would serve as honorary escorts as she is laid to rest. It was her desire that you, Miss Richardson, Paula, Frank Fisher and Mr. Reasoner be considered and treated as her family.

She further requests that you use your own judgment as to how to assist Mr. Fisher in establishing his green house and nursery business. How do you feel about her bequest, Pete?"

"You are asking how I feel, and I have no feeling. WHY DID SHE DO THIS?"

The Reverend handed to Pete one certified statement showing the birth date of the lady's son, born 30 April 1969, at Christian Services Hospital of Dallas, Texas, son of (father unnamed) and Miss Ida Strickland. Pete read it. UNBELIEVABLE! Her child born the same date as his own birthday? Then it connected! Ida Strickland was his birth mother!

Pete read the words again, then again and yet again.

"One more thing, Pete." He withdrew the chart that had been Mrs. Strickland's constant work of the heart. As he handed it to Pete, he added: "You will see her last addition to her family chart is the name of the father of her son, giving a complete history of the child's life. You are one lucky man, Pete."

Pete buried his head in his hands. Uncontrollable sobs escaped him His body shook convulsively. HOW COULD HE POSSIBLY NOT HAVE KNOWN?

The parson waited for the initial flood to subside before continuing.

"Pete your mother planned well for this event. Month after month, and year after year, her entire income was invested with the help of your father. What she left was not enough to make you a millionaire, but it certainly speaks of her attempt to allow you to be independent. We can go over those figures at a later date. I know your thoughts at this moment are fixed on your great loss.

"Your parents worked together to assure a solid future for you, and your mother, especially, wanted you to marry and have children to whom you could relate the odd circumstances which colored your life. Not too many men can have that consideration. Here are the notes I took as she dictated her wishes for her funeral. I'll leave them with you to look over. It was her wish to be buried on one side of your father with your adopted mother on his other side. I will go to the office with you to finalize those plans if you desire.

"There is one other item, Pete. Some weeks ago your mother invited me to stop by to see her. It was then she made me acquainted with the past, yours and hers. At that time she unfastened a gold chain which she always wore. She refastened it so the gold ring it secured would not be lost. It is the ring with which your parents accepted their marriage vows." He placed the envelope, with its treasure, into Pete's hand. His next words purposely uttered before Pete could utter a word.

"Right this minute, though, Pete, I would like to offer a prayer on her behalf and for your peace of mind now and later. May I?"

Without saying a word, Pete did something he had not done since childhood. He knelt on the floor and bowed his head, completely oblivious of the tears that had no end.

Kelly led the way to her apartment. Frank and Chary close behind her.

"Should we check to see what may need to be done in her apartment?" Chary needed to do something ....ANYTHING!

"Maybe we should wait until the Pastor and Pete go over things", Frank offered. One thing I can think of is to get everyone to get food together for this evening. What do you think, Kelly?"

"I think it is a wonderful idea. She was like family to everyone here. But where can we fix it to be convenient for everyone to be included? It's too cold to do anything here in the courtyard"

"How about MY PLACE? I can get tables set up and the chairs moved into the bedroom out of the way. OK?" Chary was already doing a mental count.

"Great. And, Frank," Kelly continued, "maybe you can notify everyone who wants to help. They can take food in time for everyone to visit with each other and get over the shock."

"I'm on my way. Coming, Chary?"

Kelly needed a private moment of her own. When the men left, she allowed herself the luxury of tears, and by the time Paula arrived she had showered and dressed.

"Poor Pete", she kept thinking. Not only was he grieving, but he would also feel that he was in some way to blame for the crisis. He was going to hurt for a long, long time, and she knew it.

Paula's complete absorption with her schooling would take some of the sharpness of the pain she would feel. Nonetheless, Kelly wanted to make it as easy as possible for the girl; so she prepared an aromatic bath to soften the news that had to be told.

Chary was moving furniture and stacking chairs when he saw the Reverend saying goodbye to Pete. He stepped out and. shook hands with the Parson.

"We will serve food in my place this evening. Perhaps you would care to join us?"

"Thank you, Mr. Reasoner. I will be here. And I am sure you will want to be the Soloist at the service for our friend, won't you?" The Reverend's help was perfectly timed.

Chary had not given a thought in that direction and was a bit surprised at being asked.

"IT WILL BE AN HONOR."

"Mrs. Strickland has a wonderful family here, doesn't she?"

Indeed she does, Reverend. Indeed she has."

Chapter XV

Death and love are the two wings that bear the good man to Heaven.
Michael Angelo

It was a simple service in the little church down the street. The pastor who had won the hearts of his parishioners eulogized their departed friend, speaking as much to her as to the congregation.

"On the occasion of our first snow of the last season," he began, " this group, all from the apartment complex not far from here, felt the Spirit of Christmas descend upon them. Their response was to organize a snowy parade down the center of the street to our parish doors. A delightful fellowship followed before they filed out into the dark street toward their homes. It was this diverse gathering which prompted me to ascertain their origin, and, when I learned that they were tenants in this neighborhood, I undertook to learn more of their identities. That did not require much time. YOUR FRIEND, and MINE, Ida Mae Strickland, was a member and most helpful by supplying information. In fact, a few others from there were listed on our membership list.

"On the day of their visit to these doors, one of the young ladies lingered long enough to whisper to me that she didn't know HOW TO PRAY. My response was that all people PRAY CONSTANTLY. With every fervent desire which begins in the heart and finds it's way into an expression, the urgency of that cry becomes a prayer. Sincerely uttered and felt, there is no possible outcome except fulfillment.

NOTHING BUT SUCCESS. She KNEW HOW TO PRAY. She had been praying for quite awhile without knowing it.

"This church has been taxed with debts and loss of income to such an astonishing degree that the leaders considered disbanding. Most of us were against such a move, and we had been praying to find ways to keep these doors open and to witness to all who enter herein. We have been so blessed by the attendance of this one group that we are dedicated to serving as their spiritual guide. Miraculously, so it seems, our congregation has grown in the past several months until we find ourselves serving an entire community. How wonderful are the ways of the Lord ! We. Too, are learning about the power of prayer.

"You remember that we were promised in Matthew twenty one and twenty two that All things whatsoever ye shall ask in prayer, believing, ye shall receive.

"Finally, brethren, THINK ON THESE THINGS.

"We are indebted to the young man, whose voice has been dedicated to singing the praises of the Holy Choir, for leading us into the Spiritual Uplifting which has blessed so many these past weeks. He, too, prayed; though he did not realize his desires as prayer. He so desperately wanted to sing praises to his

Maker that the music simply burst forth at the time of that blessed snow. So memorable was his perfect voice that we were prompted to invite him to join our choir. WE NEEDED HIM! We had no way of knowing that he needed us as well. But GOD KNEW!

He shared with us his earnest hope that his father might attend the upcoming concert at which his golden voice will lift us to new heights. Remember how the fatted calf was brought forth to honor the return of the prodigal son? Charles Reasoner's story is much like the one found in Luke. He was, for a time, that prodigal son. His desires became fervent prayers which were answered.

"Today we celebrate the life of Ida Strickland whose prayers have all been answered. She has served as friend and business associate to the owners of the complex in which she lived. Her love of her neighbors, her church and for the youths in her life has been rewarded with love and respect from all of them. God saw fit to answer this lady's life-long prayer to be allowed to oversee the raising of her son whom, earlier, she allowed to be adopted by a family that could provide what she could not. Her unflinching and vibrant personality and spirit will remain among us. Her influence will continue to mold characters and direct our forward growth. Let none forget the charm and warmth of Ms. Ida Strickland. She would be the first to advise us to 'SEEK FIRST THE KINGDOM OF GOD, AND ALL THESE THINGS WILL BE ADDED UNTO YOU.'

"Ida Mae Strickland is at peace now. Her prayers have been answered. As we lovingly place the body, which she no longer needs, into location of her choice, let us bless her for leaving us with beautiful memories, and be confident that this parting is only temporary. Remember the message found in John 14:2.

"'And, if I go and prepare a place for you, I will come again and receive you unto myself, that where I am, there ye may be also.' Join us in the dinning room to visit and to remember the blessing that this wonderful woman has shared with us.

In the dining room, the ladies of the church served a luncheon using several of Ida Mae Strickland's recipes; Copies were available to any who wished to have them. Amid the collection were copies of her fudge, apple dumplings, potato soup and Irish stew. Pete took copies and handed them to Kelly. She smiled and tucked them in her purse. These were bits and pieces of Pete's memory of his mother. She knew he was silently asking her to make them a part of his present life.

Then it was over....her life, his quest, and his unanswered questions...ALL ENDED!

Pete would have walked to the apartments, but Kelly matched her steps to his and suggested they acknowledge the thoughtfulness of the limousine drivers by riding with them. Once seated inside, he realized the wisdom of allowing their individual thoughts to more easily find repose. In his mind, Pete listened again to words that the Pastor had uttered, 'And if I go to prepare a place for you, I will

COME AGAIN and receive you unto myself.' The life of Ida Strickland did not cease at the ending of this one. Would he have an opportunity to erase the ugliness of his unloving thoughts toward her? Could it be that a man might again be reborn in order to right the wrongs of a previous life? What became of him if he completed the course and finally lived a perfect life? How many times would he be able to come back, and what would happen if he were never able to pay all of his back debts? He shuddered at this last thought.

The limousine stood waiting at the door of the church. The drivers were poised for courteous and reverent assistance. Kelly urged Pete to enter while she spoke to a few who were closest to Mrs. Strickland. Seeing Paula and her friend standing back from the emerging attendees, Pete motioned for the girls to join him and Kelly. Chary and Frank elected to walk the short distance. Because there was no burials held on Sunday, the final burial rite would be administered on the following day, Monday.

The young women, unaccustomed to limousine service, settled into the soft leather of their seats and would have remained quiet until Kelly opened the conversation with a question about their daily lessons. Their tensions dissolved at once, allowing for Pete to converse with his deeper self.

Mrs. Strickland had paid all of her debts in this lifetime. He concluded that she had paid the ultimate for her debts, whatever they were What a wonderful woman had been his MOTHER! He knew he needed to overcome many ills, but fewer than there might have been without her guiding hand. He could never have been worthy of her. He could NEVER have deserved her, and was sure he would NEVER forget this woman who had given him life and then given her life to guiding him. So much, SO MUCH to think about!

What about deserving Kelly Richardson? That thought prompted him to look in her direction. What a fool he had been to have entertained such undeserved jealousy! Would she ever forgive him? Could she? Hardly realizing it, his hand moved across the seat and covered her out-stretched palm.

"Will you marry me?" Pete had not intended to say that aloud. Did the words slide out by themselves? Hearing them, he wondered if they really came from his lips. He turned to face Kelly. Her face wore a question mark.

"Did you say something?" His eyebrows soared to frame his query.

"Yes, I did! I said 'Will you marry me'? She sat awaiting his answer, her face still wearing the tender question mark; her eyes twinkling their message of love.

" Kelly!" Unbelief spread its wings over his countenance.."Do you mean that?"

"Well, I don't make a habit of asking men to marry me." The excitement in her eyes matched her eager smile.

Pete was conscious of mint flavored breath escaping over her perfectly white teeth. Oh, Kelly, THANK YOU. You DO mean it, don't you? Do you think Mrs. Strickland would approve?"

"I would be very surprised if that dear lady didn't know about this long before we did. In fact, I think she may have planned her tea party we have just attended. After all she looked after you all of your life until now. I think she hopes I can handle that task for the rest of it."

The tinkling laughter from the girls drew him back to the real world. The driver's grin mirrored his approval of this happy moment. As though fearing to break such a romantic spell, the giggling grew quiet and the teenagers hands became twined together.

"Kelly, what I have wanted most in my whole life was a family...parents....and a background. I wanted to know who I am. Now, knowing my real parents were raising me, and that I was adopted by my own father, well, that's enough to convince me that this old world is being navigated by a knowing GOD. And with you, we can make our own family! That's like being born again, isn't it?" He laughed as he released her hand and pulled her into his arms.

As the limousine turned onto the circle drive at the front entrance to the apartments, Fran Seals pointed at the feline parade crossing their paths.

"Would you look at that! Max has invited some strays to help welcome us home."

This time the driver could not resist adding his obversation.

"Did you say MAX? I think you had better look again! That skinny, orange cat is leading a whole nest of orange kits. It seems the gray cat is the daddy."

Laughter elevated the somber mood and made room for a healthy acceptance of life. Grinning, yet still introspective, Pete's thoughts were uttered aloud.

"I just remembered reading something Mrs. Strickland jotted down in the corner of that precious chart of hers. I think now I understand the beauty of it.

'I am a part of every soul
Who has rambled through my heart.
And, as we approach the final goal,
We find we've traveled life together, though apart.'
Paralee K. Hoot

About the Author

Paralee Keys Hoot, a native Texan with larger than average imagination and a vocabulary to match her eighty four years, has spent her working time in many fields. COME AGAIN? is fiction which displays her rich experiences through characters the reader may meet as a part of his own family. While it is a 'feel good' love story, this fast moving tale explores the emotional paths of a diverse group of tenants in the apartment complex Pete Newman has inherited from his deceased father.

Live with them as they struggle toward goals which seem impossible to reach. Rejoice as the goals are reached in unexpected ways. Learn with them that AS A MAN THINKETH, SO IS HE.

www.ingramcontent.com/pod-product-compliance
Ingram Content Group UK Ltd.
Pitfield, Milton Keynes, MK11 3LW, UK
UKHW040559210726
13854UKWH00008B/1550

9 780759 638730